FRAMES

A VALENTINO MYSTERY

FRAMES

LOREN D. ESTLEMAN

THORNDIKE
CHIVERS

This Large Print edition is published by Thorndike Press, Waterville, Maine, USA and by BBC Audiobooks Ltd, Bath, England.
Thorndike Press, a part of Gale, Cengage Learning.
Copyright © 2008 by Loren D. Estleman.
The moral right of the author has been asserted.

The text of this Large Print edition is unabridged.
Other aspects of the book may vary from the original edition.
Set in 16 pt. Plantin.
Printed on permanent paper.

LIBRARY OF CONGRESS CATALOGING-IN-PUBLICATION DATA

Estleman, Loren D.
   Frames : a Valentino mystery / by Loren D. Estleman.
     p. cm. — (Thorndike Press large print mystery)
   ISBN-13: 978-1-4104-0860-0 (hardcover : alk. paper)
   ISBN-10: 1-4104-0860-4 (hardcover : alk. paper)
   1. Archivists — Fiction. 2. Women law students — Fiction.
3. Motion picture film — Preservation — Fiction. 4. Hollywood
(Los Angeles, Calif.) — Fiction. 5. Greed (Motion picture) —
Fiction. 6. Large type books. I. Title.
PS3555.S84F73 2008b
813'.54—dc22   2008017402

BRITISH LIBRARY CATALOGUING-IN-PUBLICATION DATA AVAILABLE

Published in 2008 in the U.S. by arrangement with Tom Doherty Associates, LLC.
Published in 2009 in the U.K. by arrangement with the Author.

U.K. Hardcover: 978 1 408 41257 2 (Chivers Large Print)
U.K. Softcover: 978 1 408 41258 9 (Camden Large Print)

Printed in the United States of America
1 2 3 4 5 6 7 12 11 10 09 08

That's part of your problem. You haven't seen enough movies. All of life's riddles are answered in the movies.

— Steve Martin to Kevin Kline,
Grand Canyon
(1991, Lawrence Kasdan and Meg Kasdan)

A NOTE TO THE READER

. . . in which the author owns up to using broad license in his description of the UCLA Film Preservation Program. The laboratory and its equipment here are state of the current art, and may in fact be either less or more advanced depending on the funds available when the book appears; and the building itself is an architectural fantasy. Certainly the size of the archival staff exceeds two, and its own offices are more modern and ergonomic. Who among us is inclined to be more sympathetic toward characters who haven't squalid conditions to rise above?

■ ■ ■ ■

I
POPCORN PALACE

■ ■ ■ ■

CHAPTER 1

You couldn't live a linear life in Hollywood. Everything was a special effect.

One moment there you were on your fleet of telephones, bellowing at brokers and bank managers, a gravel-voiced captain of industry in a screwball comedy, and then your vision swam and someone made broad circling motions on a harp, and the next moment you were lying on a stingy mattress in a rancid hotel room with a revolver in your hand.

"Tragic case," the realtor said. "Are you familiar with the details?"

Valentino nodded and took a hit from his five-dollar cup of coffee. He and the woman were standing in front of a bas-relief in bronze of Max Fink's bald sad face on a plaque in the crumbling lobby of The Oracle, a ruin left over from the lost ancient civilization of Hollywood. The floor was littered with horsehair plaster and shattered

13

chestnut shells, the plunder of some squirrel cineaste.

"Tragic, and not uncommon. He wasn't the only entrepreneur of his time to get caught in the pinch between the Wall Street crash and the talking-pictures revolution." He smiled apologetically at the realtor, Anita Somebody. "I'm a bore on this subject. Ask me how to spell DeMille and I'll recite his complete filmography."

She hesitated just long enough to convince him she didn't know DeMille from *Deliverance.* She was a carefully preserved blonde in her forties, and Valentino knew her story without asking: She'd come out from Omaha or someplace like that twenty years ago, hoping for a role on *L.A. Law,* and when that missed the mark and she couldn't get work in commercials, it was either realty or prostitution. Prostitution didn't come with a dental plan. She looked obscenely well pressed in her agency blazer and tailored skirt among the rat droppings. "It's what you call a fixer-upper," she said.

"It's what I call Ground Zero."

The grand foyer was a jungle of exposed wires and broken fretwork. An ambitious spider had erected a web of Babylonian proportions across the marble staircase and pigeons fluttered to and fro among the copper coffers in the ceiling. How the building had managed to escape demolition in a city of soaring property values and cheap Mexican labor was one for Charlie Chan.

Valentino, who knew less about construction and repair than Anita knew about Cecil B. DeMille, said, "Explain to me again why you brought me here. I'm looking for a place to live, not a lifelong hobby."

"The budget you gave us presented challenges. This neighborhood's zoned commercial and residential. No one seems to know just where the break is. Developers are reluctant to make an offer until the county board straightens it out, and the owners are anxious to sell. I'm afraid it's either this or Oxnard."

"I can't afford it."

"You haven't heard the asking price."

"I don't mean that. I love these wonderful old barns; they're in greater danger of extinction than the spotted owl. If I bought it, I'd feel obligated to restore it to its original splendor. Did I mention I'm on salary at UCLA?"

Her lipstick smile was firmer than the foundation. "Why don't you postpone your decision until you've seen all there is to see?"

"Well, I guess I can afford a tour." Saying

it, he felt an intoxicating mix of anticipation and surrender. History was his weakness and his calling.

Max Fink's very public dream of 1927 turned into a hangover two years later, but by then everyone else was too busy taking aspirins to notice.

Fink had stumbled into millions in 1912, when he rented out his candy store in Brooklyn evenings and weekends for the exhibition of silent motion-picture shorts. When he came by one night after closing and saw how many people had lined up to pay to see painted Indians chasing covered wagons across the New Jersey countryside, he evicted his tenants, bought a projector, struck a deal with a local photoplay distributor, and went into show business.

When Thomas Edison sued his movie-making competitors for infringing on his patent, Max Fink fled with them to Southern California and invented Hollywood. Along the way he stopped at choice locations to purchase vaudeville theaters in financial trouble and converted them into movie houses. Fifteen years after he sold his last Jolly Roger, he invested his profits in the stock market and used his credit to build a glittering chain of motion-picture palaces from coast to coast, saving the biggest and best for Los Angeles.

The Oracle as sketched by the architect was a Balinese-Turkish-Grecian temple, with a mild Polynesian influence and bits cribbed from Moorish Spain, Renaissance Italy, and the Gaiety Music Hall in Flatbush. Seating was designed for five thousand, with space in the pit for a hundred-piece orchestra. Fink commissioned a four-manual Wurlitzer pipe organ to accompany the action on-screen, a half-ton chandelier, and plaster Pegasuses to flank the grand staircase rising to the mezzanine. When word reached H. L. Mencken, the curmudgeonly magazine mogul quipped, "It just shows you what God could accomplish if He had bad taste."

Then *The Jazz Singer,* the Warner brothers' last-ditch attempt to rescue their studio from bankruptcy by introducing songs and spoken dialogue to the silent screen, opened to delirious throngs at Grauman's Chinese Theater. Overnight, Hollywood was forced to shut down its pantomime productions. Soundstages were erected, theaters were wired for speakers, and audiences were permitted to hear their favorite matinee idols speaking lines instead of having to read them on title cards. All this expensive retrofitting led to a recession in California.

Reluctantly — agonizingly — Fink told his contractor to reduce the size of the orchestra pit and reconfigure the auditorium to seat a paltry eighteen hundred customers. Construction in six cities was postponed until the industry could catch its second wind.

"It was like when the dot-com bubble burst in the nineties," Anita explained, in the singsong tone of a museum tour guide. "Millionaires found themselves lining up for free soup at Salvation Army missions. There was a song —" She broke off, stuck for the title.

" 'Brother, Can You Spare a Dime?' " Valentino finished. "It was about a busted railroad baron; but it applied to the Hollywood elite two years before the Depression hit New York."

"Maybe I should keep my mouth shut and leave you in charge." Anita's relentlessly chipper tone fell short of covering her impatience.

"Sorry. I *did* warn you." He reached out to stroke a crushed-velvet seat — and put his thumb through the rotted fabric. They were in the auditorium, a vast ruined chamber where the ornate brass sconces had been scavenged for scrap, leaving gaping holes in the exquisitely molded plaster.

In spite of the cutbacks, the completed

Oracle was a marvel. Fink had reduced its scope, but steadfastly refused to skimp on material or workmanship. Its marquee towered forty feet into the sky, lit by sixteen thousand electric bulbs, with colored searchlights swiveling and crossing sword-like beams far above the red-tile rooftops of Golden Age Hollywood. Attendance at the premiere of *The Hollywood Review of 1929* shattered every record set since *Ben-Hur* three years before.

Six months later, Max Fink was broke.

After the stock market collapsed in '29, he was forced to sell his theater chain to mollify his creditors. It was a temporary reprieve. In 1933, sick, penniless, and stripped of all his delusions, one of the industry's great visionaries put a pawnshop Colt to his head and blew out his brains in a dollar-a-week flophouse, two blocks down from a line of customers waiting to get in to see Mae West in a personal appearance at The Oracle. A friend who had lent him money to complete construction paid for his burial in Forest Lawn. Charlie Chaplin was among the pallbearers, who outnumbered the other mourners two to one.

"There's a quaint legend connected to the place," Anita said. "On certain nights you can see Max Fink's ghost roaming the aisles, counting the house. Bless you!"

Valentino excused himself and blew his nose into his Starbucks napkin. "I guess dust and mold spores don't affect spooks the way they do us mortals."

It was just an old building after all. Neither its backstory nor the glamorous phantasms that had glided across its screen, fly-specked now and hanging in tatters, countered the tragic truth that it should have been put out of its misery decades ago.

But Valentino was a film archivist, trained to see past such flaws as broken sprocket holes, scratched frames, and the insidious orange creep of decomposition and appreciate the glory of America's first true native art form. He found the moth-eaten carpet and water-stained gilt no less exotic than Egyptian treasures half buried in Sahara sand. There in the elephants' graveyard of spoiled dreams he experienced the same electric thrill he'd felt the day his mother took his hand and led him into a movie theater for the first time. But that had been only a whitewashed cinderblock box in Fox Forage, Indiana. This was Max Fink's fabled Oracle, home of *Hell's Angels, 42nd Street, Stage-coach,* and *Anna Christie.* He could almost hear Garbo's smoky voice, saying —

"There's a hidden staircase here."

"What?" He had to put on the brakes to avoid rear-ending the realtor. He'd followed her up the center aisle, across the apron of the orchestra pit, and back along the right wall toward the exit to the lobby. She'd stopped abruptly to pry with her fingers at a seam in the plaster. A six-foot-tall rectangular section came away, squealing on parched hinges. Dust motes swarmed up the current of air in a narrow shaft filled with steps.

"It leads to the projection booth." Anita frowned at a split nail. "Fink's crew seem to have gone to a lot of trouble to keep it out of sight."

"Illusion."

"I beg your pardon?"

"They called Hollywood the Dream Factory. A dream doesn't work if you know where it's coming from."

"Do you teach film?"

"No, the university pays me to look for them."

"Do they go missing often?"

"Since the beginning. Ninety percent of the movies made before the advent of sound are lost, mostly due to deliberate destruction back when no one thought there would be profit in reissuing them. Carelessness and neglect has seen to the rest, and it's not only silents. Poor storage conditions have decimated films made as recently as the nineteen fifties. My job is to scrounge up what's left before it vanishes."

"Huh. Well, all this gussying-up is lost on me. I just like to pop in a tape or a disc and veg out on the sofa in my sweats."

He smiled. "Bet you liked *Moulin Rouge.*"

"Oh, yes. It was fabulous! Now, watch your step. I'm sure these stairs aren't up to code."

In the stairwell he thought he smelled stale popcorn and the residue of thousands of Lucky Strikes and nickel cigars. It was probably dry rot, or possibly phantom Fink sneaking a snack and a smoke. Valentino had to turn sideways to avoid brushing the walls and soiling his shirt.

The booth was actually a spacious loft, with a square opening overlooking the remains of the screen. He remembered that The Oracle had been one of the last L.A. theaters to show 3-D movies during the brief heyday of *Bwana Devil* and *Dial M for Murder.* That process had required twin Bell & Howell projectors, each the size of a VW Beetle. They'd have needed plenty of room, but not this much. He could have put all the furniture in his apartment into this space.

Anita seemed to sense the source of his curiosity. She pointed. "There used to be a wall there. On the other side was a sort of lumber room where they stored posters and props. I probably don't have to tell you they had live shows during the Depression, to entice people who wouldn't normally spend money on a ticket. In the sixties this was a hippie commune." Her voice dropped to a whisper on the last two words, as if she were referring to a colony of lepers. "There's a bathroom through that door, which the projectionist used. It's a comfortable bachelor arrangement. Is there a *Mrs.* Valentino?"

He wondered if she was hitting on him, then discarded the thought as embarrassingly narcissistic. In any case a romantic relationship with someone who thought *Moulin Rouge* was fabulous was doomed.

"I barely have time for a private life, much less marriage. What's in there?" He pointed to a shallow alcove whose back wall curved to follow the shoulder of the roof.

"Just some cans, the flat kind they put film in. They're empty."

He felt a flash of disappointment. He'd once found two hundred feet of Theda Bara's *Cleopatra* being used to demonstrate a toy projector in a junk shop in Oklahoma City, and on first glance that place had held far less promise than this. "Is it all right if I look?"

"Be careful. The floor's in bad shape."

The enclosure was six feet wide and four deep. Stepping inside, he felt with his feet for the joists beneath the curling plywood.

"It was plastered over too," she said, "probably to conserve heat."

The air was stale but dry and cool. There was no light fixture. He peered through the dimness, groping at built-in wire racks holding jumbles of film cans that made a tinny empty noise when he moved them, a melancholy sound. He placed a hand against the cantilevered back wall to support himself and reached down to tug at the first in a row of cans standing on edge on the bottom rack.

Something thumped inside.

CHAPTER 2

"The name is Valentino."

"Yeah, right." The attendant in the campus garage, gray-haired and wearing bifocals, was old enough to assign some meaning to the name. "You look a little like him, at that."

Sadly, that was true. His light olive coloring, clean profile, and the glossy black hair that he could control only by brushing straight back from his forehead were a coincidence that caused him grief on a regular basis. In college he'd been known as Sheik, a nickname he'd likely still be suffering under if the new generation were aware there had even *been* a silent cinema, let alone a star who shared his name.

He stuck his driver's license outside his window. "Look it up on your list."

The attendant took the card and ran a thick finger down the sheet on the clipboard hanging inside the booth. He grunted and handed back the license. "Next time don't forget your parking pass."

"Thanks."

"And bring your camel."

His office was a crawl space in a building that had once been part of the university's power plant, and a reliquary of film books and piles of videocassettes, laser discs, and DVDs, with kitschy likenesses of old-time movie stars and cartoon characters in cloth and porcelain and painted tin on shelves — gifts from well-meaning friends who'd overestimated his interest in vintage cinema culture. He couldn't spend more than thirty minutes there without becoming claustrophobic, but he had part-time access to a secretary named Ruth and full-time access to Kyle Broadhead, a Film Studies professor whose name appeared in the bibliographies of half the references in Valentino's office. Broadhead occupied the room across the hall.

But not at present.

Valentino knocked, then opened the door to the little monastic cell, bare of books and bric-a-brac and Broadhead.

"He's out."

He turned to face the gray, polished-stone stare of Ruth, forted up behind her desk in the linoleum no-man's-land that separated the two offices. Every dyed-black hair was in place and sprayed stiff as vinyl, and her expression was unreadable as ever behind its enamel mask of makeup. She resembled Jane Russell circa 1943, put up in brine.

"I can see he's out," he said. "He's never out. Which hospital did they take him to?"

"The fall term began today. He makes it a point to drop in on his classroom the first and last day of the semester."

He looked at his watch. Third hour had just started. "It's too much to hope for that they'd wait till fall. I'd settle for the end of August."

"Since when do you care? You don't study and you don't teach." Which by her standards was the sum total of anyone's usefulness to academe. She herself attended a course in kickboxing two nights a week.

"Every day we see each other, he asks, 'What's new?', and I say, 'Nothing much.' The first time all year I have something worth talking about and he suddenly remembers he's faculty."

"Talk to me."

"Not you, Ms. Buzzkill."

"What's that?" Her store of vernacular had closed its doors after Sputnik.

"Someone who stands in front of the Pantages and shouts at the people waiting in line to see *The Crying Game,* 'She's a man!' "

"It was the Pacific, and I was speaking in a normal tone of voice. The fresh kid at the popcorn counter short-changed me."

"When Kyle gets in, please tell him I want to talk to him."

Her telephone rang. She snapped up the receiver. "Power plant."

Valentino kept his silence and carried it into his private space. He and Broadhead had been trying for years to persuade her to say "Department of Film Preservation" when she answered the phone. It was Ruth's opinion, frequently expressed, that an electric generator performed a more important service to the community than two grown men sitting around watching movies day after day. Apart from the fact that it was nearly impossible to dismiss an employee with her seniority, they put up with her for her inexhaustible supply of industry gossip. Her sources riddled the clerical departments of all the major studios, and she'd been around town longer than CinemaScope. Not only did Ruth know where all the bodies were buried in Hollywood; she'd helped dig some of the holes.

He opened a computer file and tried to busy himself cataloguing recent acquisitions, but they were mostly documentaries on extinct local flora and home movies of wooden oil derricks on Sepulveda and orange groves in the Valley; subjects of interest mainly to the people who wrote pamphlets for the historical society. He kept pausing to check the clock on the screen, whose second hand seemed to have contracted catatonia. After a glacial age, the door opened without a knock and Kyle Broadhead stuck his big sleepy-looking face into the office.

"Rotten feng shui," he said, dragging his gaze around the clutter. "You ought to shovel all this crap into a Dumpster."

"I need the crap. We don't all of us carry a forty-volume encyclopedia of film around in our skulls."

"What do you get from the bobble-head Popeye, memoirs of the early days at Fleischer Studios?"

"I didn't ask you in here to discuss interior decorating. I bought a theater. The Oracle, in West Hollywood. And that's not the biggest news."

The professor removed a stack of original screenplays from a plastic scoop chair and stretched out in it, almost supine with his rumpled head resting on the back and his ankles crossed, unscrewing and screwing back together the pieces of the pipe he was no longer permitted to smoke on campus. With his eyelids at half-mast and his chin drawn into the loose flesh around his neck, he looked like every musty Russian pedagogue Oscar Homolka had ever played. "Best thing you can do for that mausoleum, the humanitarian thing, would be to smack it in the kisser with a wrecking ball."

"I'm going to restore it."

"Why?"

Valentino shook his head. "For someone who spends most of his time threshing around in the past, you're incapable of nostalgia."

"There's a difference between preserving history and trying to apply CPR to a corpse. The Golden Age is always the one you missed, and you can no more bring it back than last year's lapels. Your sentiment isn't even firsthand. You're what, thirty-five?"

"Thirty-three."

"A sprout. You weren't born when places like the Oracle stopped showing first-run features. Your generation grew up watching Indiana Jones in a concrete bunker at the end of the mall."

"I have an old soul."

"My inner child is older than your old soul. Also, you've forgotten where you live. You've no concept of the bureaucratic nightmare you're about to enter. You can't comply with one ordinance without violating three others."

"I'm glad you didn't mention the cost."

"Not to mention the cost. But that's your five-thousand-pound hog and you can slop it. Don't ask me for a loan. I'm saving up for a funeral that will blow the doors off this town." He clamped the pipe between his teeth and held up his hands, like a director framing a shot. "I can see the headline in the *Mirror* now: 'Who the Hell Did He Think He Was?' "

"*The Los Angeles Mirror* folded years ago."

"My point precisely. Leave the Jurassic to us fossils."

"Anyway, I don't need your money. I knocked a hole in my savings to put down a deposit, and I've got a four-oh-one K just sitting around drawing interest."

"Drop in the ocean."

"Will Rogers told Joel McCrea to bite the bullet and buy a ranch. He said they weren't making any more real estate. McCrea died a millionaire many times over."

"No danger of that in your case. The Big One could come tomorrow and dump us all in Davy Jones's locker."

"Just as long as my check clears first. I haven't told you my big news."

31

"Bigger than going broke on the scale of William Randolph Hearst?"

"Try *Greed*."

Broadhead unclamped his pipe and pulled it apart. "This is the opposite of greed. It's financial hara-kiri."

"Not 'greed,' lowercase Roman. Think uppercase italics."

"*Greed*?"

"*Greed*."

"*Greed* as in Erich von Stroheim? *Greed* as in forty-two reels and eight to ten hours' running time? *Greed* as in thirty of those reels sent straight to the incinerator by MGM in nineteen hundred and twenty-five? That *Greed*?"

"That *Greed*." Valentino frowned. The word was starting to sound strange after so much repetition. "I take exception to the incinerator theory. There were enough cans on the rack to suggest at least four hours of footage. That's twice as much as anyone's seen in eighty years."

"Bah!" said Broadhead, and he'd never sounded more like Oscar Homolka. "You need to spend less time in the processing lab. The acetate's eating your brain."

"I don't blame you for thinking that. You've forgotten more about film than I'll ever know."

"Flattering, but inaccurate. I've forgotten nothing."

Idle braggadocio, from anyone but the author of *The Persistence of Vision,* the bible of celluloid preservation. The book chronicled Broadhead's thirty-year quest for the original 1912 version of *Quo Vadis?* produced in Italy; a quest interrupted by the three years he'd spent in prison in Yugoslavia, accused of spying. He was Valentino's only mentor. Valentino filled the old historian in on the details of his discovery.

Broadhead put away the pipe and tugged down the points of his sweater-vest, its pattern blurry beneath a layer of spilled ash. He'd been violating the university's tobacco ban for years, confident in his tenure and reputation as an ornament of the institution. "I thought *I* was a buccaneer. I never committed to buy a house on the evidence of a label on a film can I didn't even open."

"I didn't want to open one under those conditions. You know how unstable that old nitrate stock is. Also I didn't want to make Anita suspicious and hike the asking price. I made sure the contents came with the building. For all I knew, the next person she showed the place to might have been with MCA or Ted Turner. Or worse, some real-estate developer who wouldn't know Stroheim from Streisand and throw it all out. I took a leap of faith."

"Evel Knievel took a leap of faith. You jumped off the Empire State Building. Val, you've been daydreaming for years about buying one of these broke-down popcorn palaces and fixing it up. If you thought you needed an excuse, it didn't have to be the grail."

"You're right up to a point. My lease is running out and I need a place with a screening room. But I didn't imagine seeing that label. You know I'm more down-to-earth than that."

"Not on recent intelligence. As long as we're quoting the dead, you may remember what W. C. Fields said."

Valentino smiled. " 'In this town, you can't tell where Hollywood ends and the d.t.'s begin.' "

Resting his case, he propped his feet up on his desk, a thing he rarely did in the presence of his personal hero, and let Broadhead ponder while he breathed in the cramped academic atmosphere. It was alien to his own restless nature. He gave it his time in return for the heady uncertainty of never knowing when he might be called upon to abandon everything on a moment's notice and fly to Rome to retrieve a Fellini outtake or to a landfill in Alaska, quite literally to dig up the lost westerns of Thomas Ince. He had truly married adventure when he'd dropped out of film school to apprentice the ragtag team of professional scrounge artists who had founded the film preservation program. He couldn't act, direct, or write screenplays, but he could Dumpster-dive with the best.

"Everything's against it, including timing," Broadhead said. "The film was four years old when the Oracle opened. By then you couldn't give away tickets to a silent feature, so what was it doing in storage? I think your realtor salted the mine. She probably did her homework on you after you made the appointment to see the place."

"That's diabolical, even for California."

"Von Stroheim chose the title *Greed* for a reason."

"Anyway, it can't hurt to check it out. I want you to go down there with me."

"Why? I've made my pilgrimage for this term: two hundred and forty-six steps one way, and nothing but cretins with iPods on the other end. All I want to do is soak in a hot bath and watch *Survivor*. I won't be your Sancho Panza."

"I'm nervous about handling nitrate stock.

If I drop a can and the lid pops off and twenty minutes of *Greed* implodes on contact with the air, I'll wind up sticking my head in an oven. You've got decades' more experience dealing with disappointment."

Valentino took his feet off the desk. "Kyle, I don't ask you for many favors, just a point of reference now and then."

"And each point was five years of my life, not counting that shit hole in Zagreb." The professor dug out his pipe and a leather pouch nearly as traveled as he. "It's time we laid this chimera to rest. It's consumed too much money and far too many careers, starting with von Stroheim's."

"So the answer's no."

"Who said that? My God, man, it's *Greed*. Pick me up out front." He struck a match.

CHAPTER 3

Riding up La Cienega, wearing the flat tweed cap that made him look like an immigrant fresh off the boat, Broadhead sat unnaturally erect, hands gripping the dashboard and gaze fixed on the street. Suddenly he said, "Turn here!"

Valentino, ever the dutiful protégé, made the right turn onto a side street he'd passed ten times a week and had never noticed before, a narrow wandering affair with too many cars parked on it in front of small clapboard houses predating the motion-picture industry: student housing, from the ROOM TO LET signs and telltale Segway scooters parked on some of the porches. Broadhead directed him to stop before a chalky two-story with basketballs and soccer balls on the lawn like melons in a patch. The professor got out, knocked on the door, and vanished inside. Minutes later he reappeared, holding open the door for a girl to come out.

She loped toward the car. Valentino scrambled out from under the wheel.

"This is Fanta," Broadhead said.

Fanta was an athletic-looking five-ten in jeans, flip-flops, and a sweatshirt barely hanging on by her collarbone. Glistening black hair fell like a spill of graphite to her tan shoulders. Her grip was dry and firm. "I'm totally psyched, Mr. Valentino. I hope to intern with the film preservation program next summer." Self-assurance bubbled through the shallow Valley Girl voice.

"Just Valentino," he managed to say. She was stunning — and very young. "I left behind the *mister* when I crossed the state line."

She laughed out of proportion to the humor of the remark.

"Fanta breezed through the spring term with a four-point-oh," said Broadhead. "She's with the archery team. We need young muscles to carry away the booty, or pull me out when I step through a rotten floorboard. Your old soul won't answer."

"Shotgun!" She hopped in on the passenger's side.

Broadhead bent to open the rear door. Valentino put a hand on his shoulder, stopping him. "How old is Fanta?"

He frowned. "I don't know. Nineteen or twenty, I suppose. She's a junior."

"Kyle, she's named after a soft drink!"

"I don't think you're in a position to pass judgment on people's names."

"How long has it been since Elaine died?"

Understanding came up like thunder under the tweed cap. "Not that long. My God, never *that* long. What kind of old goat do you think I am? Her father was my teaching assistant my first year here. He died on the U.S.S. *Cole*."

"How much did you tell her?"

"Just that you bought a white elephant of a theater and found something of possible interest to the university. You can tell her as much or as little as you want. She's in pre-law, studying to represent the industry in cases of copyright infringement. Ethics is one of the courses she aced last spring."

"I'm sorry." Valentino withdrew his hand. "It's this town. Sometimes you see things that make you want to hire a crop duster and spray the whole place with saltpeter."

"Well, you can count me out. Elaine gave me as much in that department as a man could ever want, and devotion besides. I'd still be rotting in jail if she hadn't camped out on the State Department steps for three years."

"Forgive me."

The professor fluttered his lips rudely and unlatched the door. "Glad to see you've got something on your mind other than the flickers. There may be hope for you."

During the drive, Fanta showed a healthy interest in the scenery rolling past her window, a refreshing change from so many of her peers, who insulated themselves from the world, jabbering on cell phones and listening to music no one else could hear, over minimal headsets like the kind they gave out in coach class — "cretins with iPods," as Broadhead called them. Valentino caught her making faces at a delighted little girl in the backseat of a station wagon at a stoplight. Turning onto Roxbury Drive in Beverly Hills, he felt encouraged to conduct a guided tour.

"Wallace Beery lived there." He pointed at an estate entirely hidden behind a twelve-foot concrete wall. "He tied with Fredric March for Best Actor in nineteen thirty-two; the only time that ever happened in the history of the Academy. In real life, Beery wasn't nearly as lovable as the characters he played," he confided.

"He was a son of a bitch."

He glanced at her, startled by both the comment and its bright delivery.

"I'm a Hollywood brat," she said. "My great-grandmother was a script supervisor at MGM. 'Script girls,' they called them then." She giggled. "Jackie Cooper accidentally shot him in the foot with a prop pistol on the set of *Treasure Island.* The crew gave him a standing ovation."

Broadhead chuckled maliciously. "You don't want to go toe to toe with Fanta over antiquated showbiz gossip. She was her great-grandmother's favorite, and she listened."

"Maybe I'd be safer switching to a subject I don't know much about. Dr. Broadhead tells me you're studying copyright law."

"Kyle," Broadhead corrected. "If you can ditch your title in Lake Tahoe, I'm not going to lug mine off campus."

Valentino felt a jealous spark. It had taken him five years of close association to work up the courage to address his friend by his Christian name.

"It'll keep me off welfare for life," said Fanta, steering the conversation back on course. "Corporate's no turn-on for me, but I believe in creative rights. Camcorders in theaters, pirate DVDs in China and New York, downloading everywhere: Every time technology advances, protection of intellectual property takes a hit. Producers, directors, actors, and screenwriters are losing millions to the black market. Billions. The lawsuits are going to bitch up the courts for twenty years."

Valentino said, "I agree it's a serious problem. I just wish the studios were less easily distracted from preservation and restoration. The more established producers and directors, the film school generation, has been more than generous with donations, but funds from the front offices are drying up. The execs are so busy trying to keep the latest *Star Wars* installment out of the hands of street vendors they're letting a hundred years of history crumble to dust."

"There wouldn't be any history if the pirates had their way." Fanta's tone stiffened to Valley bedrock. "Edwin Porter went broke trying to convince judges to stop his competitors from reshooting *The Great Train Robbery* scene for scene and refusing to pay him a penny in royalties."

Valentino hesitated. "You didn't get that from your great-grandmother. She'd have to have lived to a hundred to remember it."

Broadhead said, "I consider that an insult to my teaching skills. I told you Fanta was a prize student."

"We're ganging up on him," she said, softening her tone. "If we can hit one of these big-time bootleggers with punitive damages far enough in excess of what they've ripped off, there'll be plenty to go around, for preservationists *and* the bean counters at Viacom."

"I just hope that by that time there will be something left to preserve," Valentino said.

"Amen," said Broadhead.

"Represent," said Fanta. She straightened in her seat. "Oh, too cool. Wicked."

Valentino had slowed in front of The Oracle.

He'd given his new young acquaintance credit for making her case with logic and sympathy for the opposing side. Now he assigned her extra points for her ability to see past the superficial. The old building *was* too cool, and wicked besides; but it required a special gift to disregard the ravages of time and criminal neglect to recognize its original glory.

Gone was the fabulous marquee, condemned as structurally unsound sometime between its brief Bohemian renaissance as a venue for screening obscure art films and the descent of the hippie hordes, whose unshaven armpits and community bongs had left their stench. Subsequent showings of XXX smut and blaxploitation tripe had emboldened its neighbors to obscure the

Deco fluting and baroque flourishes beneath a palimpsest of spray-painted gang symbols and schoolboy obscenities. Plywood covered the box-office windows.

"If we close our eyes, we might convince ourselves we're attending the premiere of *Gone With the Wind,*" Broadhead said. "But only if we close our noses, too. What *is* that smell?"

Valentino said, "Animal-control officers raided the place next door for breeding fighting dogs. It isn't permanent."

"Hooray for Hollywood. I wonder if Garbo will make an appearance."

"Get a clue, Professor. He hasn't taken possession yet."

Valentino could have kissed her, if he didn't think she'd sue for harassment. He looked for a place to park.

"I've seen worse, believe it or not," Broadhead said. "In Detroit, they turned one of their premier showcases into a parking garage. They ought to reinstate the death penalty for that if nothing else." He lit his pipe, mingling the scent of his apple-scented tobacco with the incense and patchouli still lingering from the Age of Aquarius. He left footprints an eighth of an inch deep in the dust on the linoleum that covered the

44

mosaic in the lobby.

Valentino, recognizing his friend's attempt to alleviate his former negativity, swallowed his resentment. A creature of indeterminate species, possibly a bat, had marked its territory inside a glass case that had once contained an assortment of Baby Ruths and Cracker Jacks. "It's a challenge," he said. "I expect to establish a lasting relationship with the Bank of Bel-Air."

"Worth every penny." Fanta caressed the plate glass preserving a letterpress poster advertising a 1979 showing of *The Rocky Horror Picture Show,* demonstrably the last feature that had played the location before a secession of fly-by-night retail shops had taken over the ground floor. She left a leopard-print impression of her fingerprints in the soot. "You should host a grand reopening with a Halloween showing of *Nosferatu.*"

"I'm going to live here, not curate a museum."

"Let's brave the stairs," Broadhead said. "I'm feeling lucky today."

Valentino had thought to bring a flashlight; the light was fading, and the projection booth was dark enough to show a feature. The beam made shadows conducive to the appearance of Max Fink's sad ghost.

"*Greed*? You're kidding me, right? Faculty doesn't usually take part in sorority initiations." Fanta studied one of the film cans in the pale orange glow.

Broadhead snatched it from her hands. He ran a thumb over the label. "Stenciling looks genuine. There's some adhesion here; they used to ship the posters stuck to the cans. Pity. An original poster for *Greed* could finance most of the renovation."

"You're killing me here," Valentino said. "You're the one who told me Hitchcock was a sadist."

"That was a compliment. No one who considered himself a master of suspense could be anything but. However, I'm not going to open them in this pest hole. We'll leave that to the nerds in the lab."

"Then why did I bring you?"

"Peer pressure, pure and simple. A historian without the support of another historian is just a geek. What's in the basement?"

Valentino was abashed. "I haven't seen the basement."

Broadhead cuffed him on the forehead with the heel of his hand. "Have you learned nothing from me in all the years we've known each other? The answer to everything is always in the basement."

"He's right." Fanta's tone was grave. "Dr.

Broadhead dissected *The Invasion of the Body Snatchers* scene for scene."

"Kyle," Broadhead corrected.

"Mercy," Valentino said. "Some of us have to live in the real world."

Broadhead said, "The more pity you. To the bat cave!"

Valentino sighed and followed them to the ground floor. After some exploration they found a narrow door leading to the subterranean reaches of The Oracle.

"*The Pit and the Pendulum,*" said Broadhead, as they negotiated the flight of slimy stairs to a part of Los Angeles Cortez himself had never laid eyes upon. Lime dripped all around like the drool of lizards employed by Roger Corman.

"*The Shining,*" furnished Fanta. "*Nightmare on Elm Street.*"

"The L.A. County building code," Valentino said. "I mean, if you really want to be scared."

At the base of the stairs, Broadhead pulled up before a life-size cutout of Mickey Rourke, advertising *9 1/2 Weeks*.

"Now, *that's* scary," he said.

They followed provocative stacks of crates, wooden and cardboard, and a depressing panoply of patching material and PVC pipe, into a room that was a shambles of loose brick and mortar, most of it accumulated at the base of the far wall. The light was dim from the surface windows in the passageway. Valentino glowered at the cracks in the wall, some of which were as wide as his wrist. Seventy-five years of earthquakes and traffic vibration had taken a heavy toll. "I hope it isn't structural."

"You used up all your hope when you bought this pig in a poke," Broadhead said.

Fanta put out an exploratory hand — and jumped back when a square yard of brick collapsed into a pile on the concrete floor. "Whoa!"

"Whoa!" echoed her voice from behind the wall.

Silence draped the three.

Broadhead broke it. "Physics isn't my field. However, when you shout into what should be eight feet of solid Southern California hardpack, it isn't supposed to shout back."

Valentino fumbled on his flashlight.

Broadhead and Fanta climbed onto the pile and began pulling pieces of rotten brick out of the edge of the hole, dropping them onto the mound. Soon the opening was big enough for a man to step through. The beam of the flash probed through and fell on rows of dusty bottles lying on their sides in a wooden rack.

The young woman — Valentino no longer thought of her as a girl — steadied herself with a hand against the side of the hole and leaned inside. "Bitchin' wine cellar. Why hide it?"

"That's not a wine cellar, child," said the professor. "It's a Prohibition stash. We just found another of Max Fink's secrets."

They entered the chamber. It was nearly as big as the room they'd left, with racks and shelves all around. The bottles they'd glimpsed were shards of empty vessels, burst where they lay, their contents evaporated. There were empty wooden cases stenciled with the names of extinct brands of Scotch and bourbon and gin. All that remained of what must have been a magnificent private stock was a faint odor of stale sour mash.

"Film cans!" cried Fanta.

Valentino slid the beam along a neat row of flat tins on a shelf near the floor, held upright by a board nailed across the heavy oaken uprights.

Broadhead slid one out. "Hold that light steady."

"I can't. My hand's shaking." He gave the flashlight to Fanta, who trained it on the lid. Broadhead blew dust off the label.

"*Greed.*" Three voices sang out in unison.

"They're numbered," said Broadhead, sliding his finger through the air along the cans on the shelf. "Twenty-five through forty-two."

"That makes a complete print, with the two dozen upstairs," Valentino said. "The full eight hours."

"Or ten. *If* it's what it says it is. This one's not empty, at least." Broadhead rattled the can in his hand. Then he looked around. "Odd thing about this room. There's no entrance except the hole we came through."

"Maybe there's a secret panel." Fanta prowled the walls with the beam. "Nope. Solid earth."

"Why wall up an empty liquor room?" Valentino asked.

"Maybe we should ask *him.*"

Fanta's voice was tight. Both men turned at the sound of it. The flashlight was shining on a human skull.

Chapter 4

The flashlight beam moved, illuminating the rest of the skeleton, heaped into a crumple at the edge of the rubble that had spilled inside the room. In the shadows it had looked like part of the broken wall.

In that moment, Valentino realized he'd never seen one "in person," and was mildly surprised to learn that it didn't look any different from those he'd seen in movies. The leering skull and hooplike ribs wore a fine coat of gray dust.

Broadhead, ever the curious scholar, leaned down and poked at a spindly upper arm with the bowl of his pipe. The bone separated from the shoulder and fell to the floor with a hollow rattle, like film clattering around the reel on a projector.

"Offhand, I'd say it's been here as long as the wall," he said.

"Duh."

They stared at Fanta, who smiled nervously and slid her hair away from her face. "Sorry, Professor. Kyle. It couldn't have gotten in here otherwise."

"I think we'll go back to 'Dr. Broadhead.' Informality seems to have bred disrespect."

"She's upset," Valentino said.

"Not really. I've seen worse on the Sci Fi Channel."

"Another argument in favor of the V-chip," Broadhead said. "We're raising a generation of emotional robots. Boo!" he shouted. Fanta and Valentino jumped. Broadhead blew through his pipe and put it away with an evil flourish. "Not so desensitized after all."

"Is this a joke to you?" asked Valentino.

"No, and it hasn't been for our friend here since before either of you was born. Me, too, possibly. Or anything else. Even tragedy has an expiration date." He turned and gathered half a dozen film cans under his arms. "Give me a hand with these. Fanta, go upstairs and bring down as many cans as you can carry without dropping them. If we're lucky, the material inside is brittle as hell."

She asked how that was lucky.

"Fragile we can deal with, if the techs are as good as their training. If it's dissolved into a mess of orange goo, we might as well put it on a salad. There's a reason it's called the Vinegar Syndrome."

Valentino stared. "We have to report this."

"Yes, and once we have, the building becomes a crime scene and everything in it becomes public property indefinitely. Would you care to see what several months in a humid L.A. evidence room can do that three quarters of a century in a relatively stable environment can't? Von Stroheim will haunt you to your grave."

"What's stable about it?"

"The air down here is cool and dry, so I have hopes for this stuff. I won't lay odds on what's upstairs. Silver nitrate's fickle. It's been known to survive under conditions that would destroy so-called safety stock, and to go up like a firecracker when someone gets a hot idea. But if it is *Greed,* we don't want some dim-witted desk sergeant mistaking it for porno and screening it at a police smoker."

Fanta said, "What's a smoker?"

Broadhead ignored her. "Everything in here belongs to the new owner until the authorities find out about Slim here. You're within your rights to remove it, and they don't need to know everything that came with the place."

"That part isn't within my rights," Valentino said. "It's — what is it, Fanta? You're the law student."

"Obstruction of justice," she said. "I'm with Dr. Broadhead."

"You're kidding."

"We don't know what killed this dude. Maybe it was natural causes, and all we have is a case of improper disposal of a corpse, by someone who's probably a stiff himself by now. If it's murder, same story. We owe it to posterity to protect a work of art from unnecessary destruction."

"Even if it means breaking the law."

"It all goes back to intellectual property rights. I'm down with it." She lifted her chin.

"Damn it, Kyle, how many young people have you managed to brainwash? You only show up two days a semester."

"Don't blame me. Your age group *invented* civil disobedience."

"Not quite. I was a little young to stage a sit-in at the dean's office in my Huggies."

"We can stand here and rock all day," Fanta said. "*Greed*'s still growing whiskers."

"Your call, Val. It's your name on the deposit check."

He didn't answer. Instead he stepped over and started picking up film cans.

"That's my boy. Carpe diem."

"Totally." Fanta headed for the stairs.

■ ■ ■ ■

"Sergeant Clifford, West Hollywood Homicide." The woman stooped to shake his hand in the room outside the formerly hidden chamber. Considering her height and her startling green eyes and red hair, teased out in an '80s do, he wondered what circumstances had led her to choose law enforcement over modeling. She was beautiful enough for the movies, but too tall for most of the leading men. "You're the owner?"

"Valentino." He braced himself at the question he saw coming.

"The fashion designer?"

He hesitated. "No, the silent film star. I mean, that's who most people mistake me for. Actually, I'm not related to either of them." He was babbling. He shut himself up.

She looked at his business card. He'd given it to one of the two officers in uniform who'd been first on the scene. "Says here you're a film detective. I thought I knew all the bureaus."

"It's just a jazzy name for a procurer. This is a showbiz town. I'm a consultant with the Film Preservation Department at UCLA."

"Theaters?"

"Movies. This started out as a search for a house with a screening room."

"Did you know a corpse came with the place?" Clifford smiled girlishly, but her eyes were as sharp as emeralds.

"If he had, he'd have tried to bargain down the price," said Broadhead, coming to his rescue. He introduced himself and grasped the sergeant's hand. "I teach film at the university."

She turned to Fanta. "And what do you do, sell popcorn?"

Valentino noticed that the sergeant listened to the answers to all her questions without making notes. Various personnel, in and out of uniform, flowed past the quartet in both directions, carrying cases and bizarre paraphernalia. Someone had erected a trouble light inside the room containing the skeleton and trailed twenty-five feet of orange extension cord out into the passageway. Lightning pulsed from flash equipment on the other side of the ruined wall.

"So you're all in pictures, more or less," said Clifford.

Broadhead said, "More less than more. We're not affiliated with any of the studios. We're academics."

"Teachers' salaries must be improving.

This place had to have cost a bundle."

"I only put down a —"

Broadhead interrupted. "Do you consider him a suspect in a seventy-year-old death?"

Her green gaze shot his way. "What makes you say seventy?"

"It's been that long since they repealed Prohibition."

"These bricks haven't been up nearly that long. Not all of them. Those yellower ones weren't available before the fifties. See, they form a rectangle, and they're not rotten like the section you pulled down. My husband's in construction," she said. "He talks about his work. He has to, if we're going to have any sort of chitchat. I can't exactly bring my office home to dinner."

In the light spilling out of the room being investigated, Valentino could clearly see the contrast. He remembered Broadhead's earlier concern. "There was a door."

"Someone walled it up. It's easy to guess why. Our criminalist confirms a later date of death; something about the fillings in the teeth." She caught Valentino's face brightening. "Normally this kind of talk upsets people."

He'd been thinking, *A film older than the building, and a corpse younger. They can't be connected.* He felt himself turning color. "I found it interesting. A lot of the films I screen are murder mysteries."

"Mm-hm. Man who's seen as many pictures as you, I guess you're not squeamish about skeletons."

"I still flinch when Lon Chaney's mask comes off in *The Phantom of the Opera*."

"That one I know. I saw the road show when it played L.A. Come in and take a look. Maybe you can give us a positive ID, ha-ha."

A flash tripped just as Valentino stepped over the rubble and into the room. The on-cue timing made him feel as if he'd entered a live set; which, he supposed, was what it was. He had the sensation that the man with the camera, the uniformed officer scribbling in his report book, the pair of technicians mixing and applying their powders, the woman in the green smock bent over the pile of bones in the corner had all been running their lines and primping only a moment before, waiting for the director to take his seat in the canvas chair.

He decided that when this was over he should put in for a vacation that didn't involve a hotel room with a movie channel.

"Ms. Johansen, a minute?" Clifford asked.

The woman in the smock sat back on her heels. She wore a cuplike mask over her nose and mouth. When she took it off, Valentino was struck by her features. She was a short-haired honey blonde with elliptical blue eyes, clear and unflawed. Her nose was straight and she had a generous mouth that looked as if it might contain a smile as bright as a klieg. Her looks were exotic, unlike Clifford's conventional beauty, yet entirely American.

She wasn't smiling. "A minute is an hour. What's so important? Oh, hello." She noticed Valentino and moderated her scowl.

"Hello," he said. "I didn't think bacteria would be a problem after so many years."

"What? Oh, the mask. I'm allergic to dust." She sneezed.

"Isn't that like a jockey who's afraid of horses?"

"Most cases don't lie around this long waiting for attention. Even cold cases."

Clifford said, "Mr. Valentino owns the building. Harriet Johansen, with the criminal-science division. I told you what she said about the deceased's fillings."

"Forgive me for not shaking hands." She held up a miniature whisk broom in a rubber glove.

He looked past her. The trouble light shed halogen on the skeleton, which properly was no longer a pile of bones but now lay

59

stretched out on its spine. Many of the segments had separated, but Ms. Johansen or someone had arranged all the parts according to their original locations. He figured she'd be a whiz at jigsaw puzzles. There was a musty odor under the ancient liquor smell in the room that reminded him of old magazines.

"What else have you got?" Clifford asked.

"He was about a thirty-two short, not much over five feet with his skin on. I can do a more precise measurement back at the lab, and C.G. should take care of the rest."

C.G. stood for *computer generation.* Valentino knew that much from Cyber Age movie magic. "How do you know it was a he?"

"Shape of the pelvis. Also I caught him looking down my blouse when I bent over."

He grinned. "Was it murder?"

"Tell you when I finish dusting, maybe. If there was bone trauma, a skull fracture, or a blade or a bullet nicked a rib, yes. Without that, or a loose slug coming to light when we move the cadaver, all we've got is —"

"Improper disposal of a corpse," Valentino finished.

"Hey, you swiped that from me."

He turned at the sound of Fanta's voice. He hadn't even been aware she and Broadhead had followed him into the room. He made introductions. The reality of his proprietorship had only sunk in when Sergeant Clifford referred to him as the owner. Playing the host seemed appropriate.

Ms. Johansen said hello and sneezed again. "Excuse me."

"Bless you." All four spectators spoke at the same time.

Clifford said, "Any sign of clothing?"

"Not a scrap, and he hasn't been here long enough for leather and fabric to decompose completely. That takes more than a century, under outdoor conditions. The building isn't that old, and as I said his dental work postdates construction by thirty years at least."

"A stripped body spells murder to me," said the sergeant. "What else?"

"Ask me downtown in a day or two." The criminalist peeled off her gloves. "You can tell the morgue team to bag him up anytime."

Valentino straightened. His back was sore from crouching, on top of helping carry more than forty cans of old celluloid up and down stairs and loading them into the trunk of his car. He was nervous about leaving them in that uncontrolled climate for long.

He asked Clifford if she had any more questions.

"Just one. What was removed from that shelf?" She pointed at the rack that had contained the film. "The dust is spread evenly everywhere but there."

Her steely tone, and that emerald stare, got to him. He took in his breath to confess. Broadhead gave him a sideways kick in the ankle. "Ouch!"

Nothing good can come from underestimating a cop's peripheral vision. She swung her attention to the professor. "What was that?"

"Restless Leg Syndrome." His face wore no expression.

Just as she lifted an authoritative finger, a whey-faced plainclothesman Valentino had seen drifting in and out interjected himself into the group. "Media's here, Sarge."

"How many?"

"Three stations and the cophouse guy from the *Times*."

"The gangs in East L.A. must be on vacation." She stuck the finger at Valentino. "I've got your contact information. We'll talk."

The three civilians migrated toward the jagged exit. Harriet Johansen, packing her whisk broom and other assorted tools into a black steel case, stuck her striking face into a tissue and sneezed again.

"Bless you." This time, Valentino was the only one to say it.

She wiped her nose and smiled up at him. He'd been dead right about the candle-power. "Thank you."

Broadhead gave him a push. "Move it, Don Juan."

"That was Douglas Fairbanks," Valentino corrected.

Chapter 5

Valentino broke the silence of several blocks. "Restless Leg Syndrome?"

"It's a real condition," Broadhead said. "Look it up."

This time, the professor sat in the front passenger's seat while Fanta rode in back. Valentino had had to maneuver the car out of a tight space between satellite trucks double-parked in front of The Oracle. Evidently, the discovery of a vintage corpse was of sufficient human interest to attract the press to a crumbling landmark.

"Clifford's not an idiot," he said. "She knows we're hiding something."

"Not evidence," Fanta put in. "Not technically. The film had to have been there since before the theater changed hands the first time, long before whatever happened happened. Connecting the two would be an impossible case to make in court."

"That's for the police and prosecutor to

decide. I'm not comfortable with lying to them."

"You didn't," Broadhead said. "I did, to prevent you from blurting out a truth that could destroy a seminal artifact from the first quarter-century of the cinema. I went to prison for less reason than that. At least the L.A. County Jail has central heating."

"If you think I'd let you go to jail while I kept silent —"

"That's for *me* to decide." He filled his pipe. "*Greed* and I are near contemporaries. I've made most of the contributions to our common purpose I'm ever likely to, but that film, that wonderful crackbrained child of a mad genius, hasn't even started. Irving Thalberg never gave it the chance. It doesn't take a Ph.D. to determine which sacrifice is better."

Fanta rapped her knuckles on her window-sill. " 'We, the jury, find the defendant not guilty on the grounds of common sense.' "

"All the same, if Sergeant Clifford asks me again about that empty shelf — and she will — I'm going to tell her, Restless Leg Syndrome or no."

Broadhead got his tobacco going and opened his window to expel the smoke. "All I ask is that you stall long enough for us to look at the McGuffin and if it's what we hope it is, strike off a new negative on safety stock. After that she can T.P. the squad room with it if she likes."

"That'll take weeks! I can't put her off that long."

"How is it done?" Fanta leaned forward in her seat. "I don't guess it's like copying a tape or burning a disc."

"Not with film," Broadhead said, "and certainly not with anything as volatile as silver nitrate. Silver's the culprit; the very stuff that made the silver screen sparkle. It's a corrosive agent, carrying the seeds of its own destruction. You have to expose it onto new stock a frame at a time."

Valentino said, "That's thousands of frames. In this case hundreds of thousands. You measure forty-two reels in miles, not feet."

Broadhead chuckled. "Thalberg called von Stroheim a 'footage fetishist,' just before he ordered the editors to cut it to two hours' maximum running time. After months of shooting on location in San Francisco and Death Valley, and part of the cast still in the hospital, the studio scrapped seventy-five percent of the feature."

"Possibly eighty," said Valentino. "No one ever sat down and watched the whole thing with a stopwatch."

"Professor, you're going to have to refresh my memory on who Irving Thalberg was."

"Head of Production at MGM. Second in command to Louis B. Mayer, the *M* that roared."

She slumped back in her seat. "Fascist company freak."

"People are too harsh on him." Valentino detoured around barricades on Wilshire. Gaffers were inflating a huge bag for a stunt jumper standing on the roof of Bullock's Department Store to land on. You couldn't drive a straight line across the city without running into an accident or a film shoot. "Thalberg greenlighted most of the studio's greatest projects in the early years, including *The Big Parade,* often over Mayer's objections. He was the inspiration for F. Scott Fitzgerald's last novel."

"It's so hard to tell the good guys from the bad guys in this business," she said.

Broadhead ground his teeth on his pipe stem. "That's why they made the movies they did, where you could tell them easy."

Valentino said, "It's a hard sell, piecing out evidence to the police. I should run it past Henry Anklemire."

"You mean Smith Oldfield," Broadhead corrected. "He's in the legal department. Anklemire's Information Services."

"I mean Anklemire. Who better than an ad flack to make a difficult sale?"

"Just don't let the ignorant little motor-mouth into our building. When we finished restoring *Johnny Tremain* last year, he wanted to invite Walt Disney to the first public showing."

"That's no reason to put him off limits."

"When I told him Disney's heirs had him cryogenically frozen in nineteen sixty-six, he said, 'Gee, it'd be swell if we could thaw him out in time for the reception.' "

"He was right." Fanta met Valentino's gaze in the rearview mirror. "Think what it'd do for contributions."

Broadhead told her she was going to make a fine intern.

When they turned onto her street, she said, "Hey, don't drop me off. I want to see what goes down with *Greed*."

"Those lab nerds don't excite as easily as we do," Broadhead said. "They'll just sign it in, seal the cans, and stick them in the fridge. Then that little gnarled gnome of a librarian will insist on assigning it a priority at the bottom of a list of fifty other projects. Fortunately, the president of our illustrious institution has been after me for a year to get Francis Ford Coppola to speak at next year's commencement, and Francis owes me a solid. That'll nudge it to the top."

"Bogus Byzantine bullshit. I'm glad I'm studying law."

Valentino stopped in front of her house. "It's been a real pleasure, Fanta. We'll let you know as soon as we find out. Meanwhile —"

"I know: Cool out. It's like my first professional consultation, with attorney–client privilege and whatever. They won't hear" — she uncased a smile that still showed the impression of braces — "boo!" She got out and waved at them from the porch.

Both men were still grinning as they pulled away. "I see the attraction," Valentino said.

Broadhead's face went sour. "That's less funny now than when you thought it was genuine. Her old man was the best T.A. I ever had. He'd be an assistant professor by now if he hadn't answered the call to duty." He tipped open the dashboard ashtray and knocked his pipe out into it. "What's the name of that big red dog in newspaper cartoons?"

"Clifford." Now Valentino frowned. "She's big, and she sure is red, but there were no dogs in that room."

"That criminalist was pretty cute. You're one to talk about academics in heat."

"It was the forensics I was interested in. I spent three weeks in northern Michigan tracking down the home movies Preminger shot on the *Anatomy of a Murder* set."

"You should open with that next time you see her. It's better than candy and flowers."

"Okay, we're even." Valentino left the Beverly Hills city limits, and with them that subject. "What do you think of the skeleton in my closet?"

"Nothing I hadn't seen before. I took a shortcut through the Roman catacombs on my way to *Quo Vadis*."

"I mean the murder. If that's what it was."

"If you're worried about the Big Red Dog, don't. The pressure to solve a crime more than four decades old ranks right up there with our obligation to restore *Francis the Talking Mule*. The TV morons will stop playing it up the minute some former kid actor gets arrested for beating up a transvestite, and the cops will move on."

"That's not what I'm worried about. Well, I am, but that's not why I brought it up. It's an occupational hazard, I guess. There's a fine line between scrounging up ten feet of early D. W. Griffith and sleuthing out a felon."

"You've fallen victim to your own PR. I told you I disapproved of putting that *film detective* tag on your business cards. I bet you got that from Anklemire."

"Guilty. But that doesn't mean it was a bad decision. *Archivist* doesn't open many doors."

"Speaking of doors, you're about to drive past the one to our place of business."

Valentino signaled and turned abruptly into the North Campus entrance. The monster Hummer behind him screeched its brakes and blared its horn.

"Bummer," Broadhead said. "Now we've made an enemy of Governor Schwarzenegger."

The gray-haired parking attendant glared through his bifocals at Valentino. "Who're you now, Ramón Novarro?"

"I haven't been home to pick up my parking pass," Valentino said. "Mea culpa."

"I guess you Hollywood libs think that's funny." The attendant raised the gate. "My sister's a nun, and my boy's at the seminary."

"Sorry." Valentino drove through.

"First the cops, now God," Broadhead said. "Man, you're screwed."

"Don't *you* have a parking pass?"

"Our beloved department head got it revoked. He's got a lease on an SUV the size of Sacramento and I drive a nifty little

71

hybrid that gets a hundred and sixty miles to the gallon. He thinks I wrote in Stalin in the last presidential election. There's a spot, next to that midlife-crisis Corvette."

They parked. Valentino said, "We can't carry more than twenty cans between us. We'll have to make two trips."

"Why take chances with our creaky knees when burly undergrads come twenty cents a pound? We'll come back with two of them and a couple of cartons from Office Max."

"That's like transporting the relics of a saint in a White Castle sack."

The professor shook his big shaggy head. "You're too reverent, like our friend in the parking booth. I earned my first dollar in this profession pedaling reels of *Wings* between Toledo and Sylvania, Ohio, on a bicycle. I logged a hundred miles a night between showings."

"How old *are* you, Kyle?"

"I could tell you, but then I'd have to kill you. This university has a mandatory retirement policy. I don't play golf, and fishing bores me till I bleed."

"It wouldn't be that much of a culture shock. You don't teach more than four hours a year."

"Those four hours entitle me to use the film library and reference sources, which is what I do with the rest of my time. I'm writing a book at last."

"You wrote a book. *The Persistence of Vision*." He wondered, with a prick of apprehension, if his friend's memory had begun to fail. Even the most impressive and efficient machinery broke down with time. He opened his window, letting oxygen into the stuffy car.

"That was a coffee-table decoration. I was a sprout in my fifties when I threw it together, blathering on for page after page about material I'd never seen because it had been dead or buried for a generation. Speculation and hearsay, the coronary and cancer of serious scholarship." He sighed bearishly. "I wish flashbacks existed offscreen. I'd revisit that benighted period and horsewhip myself. Next best thing is to prepare a second edition; denounce my adolescent exhalations and set the record straight based on what's come to light since sliced bread. It's almost finished."

"When do you write? You come in early, go home late, and I never see you at your computer or even scribbling on a piece of paper."

"It's all here." Broadhead tapped his bulbous brow. "The rest is scutwork."

"The scutwork is what takes most of the

time. What about notes?"

"Scratch, scratch, scratch. These old knuckles are too stiff. But my cerebral cortex is covered with shorthand."

"But what if you don't live long enough to share it?"

"I am sharing it." He reached across the console and patted Valentino's knee. "Let's go find those undergrads before that stuff in the trunk reaches the third stage of decomposition."

"What if it has already?"

"Then we have all the time in the world. Unless, of course, it blows up."

CHAPTER 6

"Herr Valentino, you have had your rest, *ja?"*

He started awake; he thought. Afterward he wasn't sure. A swatch of moonlight lay on the bedroom carpet like a gauntlet flung to the floor. A dark figure stood in the shadows to one side of the window.

Valentino's heart flopped over. Had he locked his door?

"You will save *mein Kindling, ja?* I am counting on you."

The intruder's guttural accent — his "will" sounded like *vill,* his "save" like *safe* — was as hard to follow as his German. The man in the bed had the wild thought that his apartment had been broken into by a neo-Nazi skinhead. All kinds of fanatic roamed the streets of Century City late at night, along with garden-variety burglars and gangbangers off their turf.

"My wallet's on the bureau." His voice wobbled. "There's some video equipment in the living room. Please take them and go."

A bitter laugh escaped the shape in the shadows. It chilled the listener with its mercilessness and strange familiarity. He recognized it but couldn't place it.

"What do I want with your trinkets and money? I spent more than you earn in a month on one dinner at the Trocadero. I want *mein Kindling*."

Vot do I vant; it was maddening, that voice, so well known and yet just outside the grasp of memory, like a character actor in an old movie. That sparked a flash, but it faded before he could bring it into focus.

The Cafe Trocadero had been gone fifty years, along with most of the stars, directors, and cigar-chomping moguls who had dined there. *Mein Kindling?* He scrambled to remember his high-school German. *My child, my beloved child.*

"I think you've mistaken me for someone else. Another Valentino." It sounded weirdly comical, even to him. He'd begun to believe he was dreaming. He'd fallen asleep straightaway after the long day of investment, discovery, elation, shock, and guilt.

"*Du lieber Gott!*" roared the stranger. He stamped his feet twice in a goose step, thrusting himself into the shaft of cold light and halting with a click of his heels like a pistol shot.

Valentino's breath caught. The man was dressed head to toe in the uniform of an imperial Austrian officer. A visored cap perched at an arrogant angle above his shaved temples, his white tunic was buttoned to his throat and spangled with medals, and riding breeches were stuffed into the tops of gleaming black knee-length boots. In one hand he held a pair of gloves, in the other a leather riding crop, its braided-thong handle resting against one shoulder like an army rifle. A monocle glittered in one eye and a cigarette smoldered in a long holder clamped between his teeth.

Erich von Stroheim. *Foolish Wives,* 1922; one of his frequent turns in front of his own cameras. It came to Valentino as clearly as if he were looking at a black-and-white publicity still.

In the brief silence, he felt his heart rate slowing. His fear lapsed into annoyance. Not a ghost or even a dream, but a practical joke, and he recognized the hand that had fashioned it. So they hadn't been even after all.

"Nice costume," he said. "Tell Kyle you accomplished your mission. Where'd he reach you, through your booking —"

"Silence!" The riding crop whistled through the air and struck one of the shining boots with a crack. "You will save it, or I will see that you never work in this town again."

Valentino forced himself to meet the iron gaze. A nerve twitched in a closely shaven cheek, branded by a thin white cicatrix like a Heidelberg dueling scar. It seemed to him the monocle had misted.

A bell rang. Von Stroheim looked up as if he'd heard an air-raid siren — then vanished. The shaft of moonlight fell uninterrupted to the carpet.

The noise continued, a harsh insistent sound, more buzzer than bell. Valentino sat up as if jerked by a wire. Sunlight filled the room. He reached over and smacked the button on his alarm clock. The buzzing stopped. The digital face read 7:31. Time to get up.

He put on his robe and prowled the bedroom, looking for wires and projection equipment, not yet prepared to believe he'd dreamt the encounter. He hadn't had so vivid a nightmare since the night his mother had taken him to see *Alien* (Rated R; what could she have been thinking?) and he'd awakened screaming, certain a hideous extraterrestial beast had erupted from his abdomen.

There was no sign of a prank, high-tech or otherwise, there or in the living room, dominated by a forty-eight-inch rear-projection television, VCR/DVD combo, surround-sound tuner, and speakers. An unexpected bonus from his department head for his part in recovering the lost courtship footage from the 1954 version of *A Star Is Born* had started him thinking of getting a flat-screen TV, or even installing a digital projector and state-of-the-art screen, but then his landlord had told him he was raising the rent after Valentino's lease ran out in December. That was what had set him on the house hunt.

Well, if anything could fill a man's head with startling images, the decision to commit to a white elephant in West Hollywood and the simultaneous discovery of both a legendary lost masterpiece and mysterious human remains more than qualified. *"Mein Kindling"* was, of course, the late director's brainchild, butchered and cast aside by the studio. Rescuing it from destruction had been uppermost on Valentino's mind when he went to bed. It would have been unusual *not* to have conjured up something weird in his sleep.

Thirty minutes later, bathed, shaved, and dressed in California casual, he left for work. By the time he'd stopped for his morning jolt of Starbucks, the ghost of Erich von Stroheim had vanished from his thoughts nearly as thoroughly as it had from his bedroom.

"God, I love foul play!"

Henry Anklemire leaped up from behind his desk next to the boiler room in the basement of the administration building. The assistant director of Information Services was an evil cherub in one of the toupees he bought from Nicolas Cage's hairdresser when the star was through with them and a checked suit (size portly), polka-dot tie, and striped shirt that made a cataclysmic statement his visitor thought could not have been coincidental. His face glowed as from a strong shot of whiskey.

"We'll just keep that between ourselves," Valentino said. "My department head thinks Sherlock Holmes was a sociopath. He prefers things orderly and without mayhem."

"I know from bosses." The little flack twirled a finger beside his temple. "Meshuggener, and besides that depressing to be around. I could've had a nice comfortable space down the hall from the director's, with a window yet. I said, no thanks, I'll curl up down here with the rats and spiders. All those downer vibes can crush a man's spree de corpse."

"I heard that was the director's decision."

"Who cares where an idea came from if it's good?" Anklemire was on a roll. "Murder and malice, yum. Look at Marilyn Monroe; not one-tenth the talent of Judy Holliday, but she had the good sense to get herself killed by the Kennedys. You ever see Judy Holliday on a T-shirt?"

"There's some question about whether she was murdered, and whether the Kennedys were involved. And you wouldn't know Judy Holliday from Doc Holliday if I hadn't forced you to watch *Born Yesterday* on DVD."

The little man was younger than he looked. Male-pattern baldness and a high-pressure career on Madison Avenue had aged his appearance, but the spring mechanism that propelled his thoughts and actions remained intact. Retired in his thirties on a medical disability (pernicious hemorrhoids; although Kyle Broadhead insisted the surgeons had kept the hemorrhoid and thrown away the patient), he had offered his marketing savvy to the university on condition that his salary wouldn't threaten his Social Security benefits. The director of

Information Services had assured him that low pay was no obstacle to his employment.

Broadhead wasn't alone in his opinion of Anklemire. Most of the administration and faculty loathed him for the very reasons Valentino liked him. He was an aggressive promoter who knew the common denominator that shook loose money from every area of society, and he had no patience for questions of propriety or prestige. Give him a salable commodity and he'd sell it. Give him a dead dog with live fleas, and he'd sell that too. He knew nothing about movies or their history, but he knew how to turn silver nitrate into gold.

"*Born Yesterday.* Great flick. They ought to colorize it. What you want to do, you want to send the picture — what's it called again?"

"*Greed.* But that's not what I —"

"I like it. One-word titles pop: *Porky's, Rambo, Caddyshack.* Big-time boffo box office. And when you stick a Roman numeral on the end: Kaboom! Blockbuster. Any chance of a sequel?"

"I sincerely doubt it."

"Well, you can't always get cream cheese with your bagel. You want to send the picture on tour, book all the revival houses, pass the hat for donations. Then you bring it out on disc. This outfit sure can use the cash." He raised his voice above the banging of the water pipes next door. "What we do to get them in is play up the murder mystery angle. Dust off some retired forensics geek to C.G. what Mr. Bones might've looked like when he was walking around, air it on *America's Most Wanted.* Make sure *Greed* gets a mention, run a thirty-second clip. See the movie, catch a killer, get a reward. Can't miss."

"We may have found a great film that's been missing for eighty years. Isn't that worth anything?"

Anklemire exposed gold teeth in a yawn. "Strictly third paragraph. Below the fold and after the sports and weather. Nobody cares."

"Nobody but the people you and I work for." But he didn't argue. The assistant director's opinion sadly reflected the majority's. "If it turns out to be *Greed,* I'll come back for this lecture. What I need is to spin the situation so the LAPD doesn't seize the film for evidence before we can strike off a safety print."

"Who's the cop?"

"Sergeant Clifford, with West Hollywood. I don't know her first name."

"A broad. Why'n't you say so in the first

place? Send her flowers."

"That's the dumbest, most offensive thing I've —"

"Relax, Doc. I was speaking metaphysically."

"Metaphorically." He didn't bother to set him straight on *Doc.* To the little man, everyone at UCLA not connected with the administration was faculty. He watched Anklemire circle behind his desk, sit down, and use his handkerchief to snap a piece of lint off one of his Italian loafers. What he saved on his clothes and hairpieces he spent on shoes.

He poked the handkerchief back into his pocket and fussed with it until it blossomed like a poppy. "You eggheads are sitting on the best chick magnet in Southern California and you never get laid. You got like a billion dollars of snazzy equipment there in the lab, but you don't show it off. You said Broadaxe mentioned turning the dingus over piece by piece?"

Valentino was sure Anklemire knew the name was Broadhead. "If by dingus you mean *Greed,* yes. But —"

"Soften her up. Blind her with bling. All them computers and electronic microscopes and projectors and that gizmo that stamps and stacks discs, guys waltzing around in haz-mat suits, it's *Willie Wonka Meets Doctor No.* Did I get that right?" The glint of insecurity faded before his listener was sure he'd seen it. He nodded.

"When she's impressed, hit her with the proposition."

"It can't be as simple as that."

"It's a simple world. Somebody has something to sell, somebody else is looking for something to buy. I made a nice little commission for years bringing 'em together. She call you yet?"

"Not yet. Should I wait?"

"No. Don't buy that BS the feminists shovel out. Broads like it when you make the first move."

"Are you married?"

"No, I've been in advertising all my life. Call her."

"I'm trying to stay out of jail, not ask for a date."

"You're asking for a date, all right. You're just not picking her up or paying for dinner. Call her." He picked up his telephone, standard, receiver, and all, and banged them down on Valentino's side of the desk.

"I'd better run it past Dr. Broadhead first. At this point we don't even know what we're trying to protect. We haven't unwrapped it yet."

"Don't stall too long, that's my advice. If she calls first, your odds get cut in half." He bounced his crossed leg up and down, admiring the shine on his toe. "What?"

Valentino realized he was staring at him. "Did you ever happen to read a book called *What Makes Sammy Run?*"

"What is it, a bio of Sammy Davis, Jr.?"

"Not quite. You might want to check it out. There's someone in it you might recognize."

"Well, I hope it's short. I waded through three hundred pages of that *Day of the Locust* deal you gave me and didn't see so much as a cockroach." He uncrossed his legs and crossed them the other way. The man simply couldn't keep still; Valentino wondered if it was the hemorrhoids. "If this *Greed* turns out to be the McCoy, get me what you can for the campaign."

"Such as?"

"You're the archaeologist. Start digging. I can't write copy without material."

"Archivist, not archaeologist."

"What's the difference?"

"Not a lot."

"Do your homework, Poindexter. Interview people. Get me color: crazy directors, bootleg booze, wild parties in big houses on Sunset. Voh-doh-de-oh-doh!" He jogged his upper body, elbows out. He was a living video arcade.

"Who do you suggest I interview? Von Stroheim's been dead almost fifty years and time hasn't been any kinder to the rest of the cast and crew." He was glad he hadn't said anything about last night's dream. Anklemire would have had him stalking the ghost around like a paparazzo.

"There's always somebody, or if it isn't somebody it's somebody's son or grandson. Nobody blows through this town without leaving something behind: diaries, letters, pirate maps, arr! Get me something I can use to sell popcorn."

"That I can do. I'm not sure about *America's Most Wanted*."

"Yeah. On second thought, a mystery's no good without a solution. People just get pissed when you get their curiosity all worked up for bubkes."

Valentino laughed. "What do you want me to do, solve the case?"

"If it isn't too much trouble."

■ ■ ■ ■

II
DOUBLE FEATURE

■ ■ ■ ■

CHAPTER 7

He found Ruth at her desk, limning a set of bright orange fingernails in yellow from a tiny bottle on the blotter. They looked like candy corns; further proof, he thought, that the ability to distinguish colors deteriorated with age. "Dr. Broadhead's been asking for you." She didn't look up from her project.

He started toward Broadhead's office.

"Not there. In the projection room at the lab. He wants to show you something."

He felt a thrill of anticipation. Then he reminded himself the techs couldn't have finished duplicating enough footage of *Greed* (if it was *Greed;* he kept having to remind himself not to build up hope) to screen more than a couple of seconds. The shriveled little sourpuss who had signed it in the day before hadn't inspired him to think they'd get to it right away. "Did he say what it was?"

"No, and I didn't ask. Something old and

musty and full of dead people, what else? I suppose you're going to waste another fine California day watching movies."

The sky that morning looked like bad tapioca pudding. Several school districts had canceled classes in response to a smog alert.

"Why don't you join us?" he asked. "Admission and popcorn are free."

"The last time I went to a private screening, David O. Selznick chased me around the pool."

"We'll try to restrain ourselves. Is there *anything* about movies you approve of?"

She blew on her nails. "They're shorter than most baseball games."

"Baseball too? What about apple pie?"

"I never eat dessert."

"Why do you work here, Ruth? You must be miserable all the time." Which would explain a great deal.

"It's better than my third marriage. He played shortstop for the Dodgers; that's what brought him out here from Brooklyn. That's why I don't like baseball." She looked up at him. Her face was like fine painted china. He had the impression that if someone struck it, it would crack apart, like Vincent Price's in *House of Wax*. She said, "You're young, it doesn't matter how many hours you waste, day after day. A man Dr. Broadhead's age ought to make the best of the time he has left."

"What *is* Dr. Broadhead's age?"

"If I had to go by how he looked when I came in, I'd say a hundred and fifty."

"He was here when you came in? Even he never makes it that early."

"He never went home. He was here all night." She screwed the cap back on the bottle of polish adeptly, sparing contact with her nails. No arthritis there. "It's not healthy to keep so much company with dead people. That comes soon enough."

Valentino went to the laboratory building, a sleek example of ultramodern architecture more in keeping with *Angry Red Planet* than West Coast Ivy League. Through the thick glass inside he saw technicians working in the lab, in smocks and shiny neoprene gloves, some wearing hoods to protect them from the toxic fumes coming from film in the third stage of decomposition and beyond — haz-mat suits indeed, as Anklemire had said. Valentino thought fleetingly of Harriet Johansen in her breathing mask. He couldn't forget her smile, once he'd finally coaxed it into the open.

"There you are." Broadhead sounded irritated. "When did you start keeping banker's hours?"

The professor had just stepped into the hall from the projection room, as if he'd been waiting at the open door. He looked more unpressed than usual in the clothes he'd worn the day before. His face sagged like a deflated balloon. He looked a hundred and fifty easy.

"I had a meeting with Henry Anklemire. Ruth said you were here all night. I thought you were going home to take a bath and watch *Survivor.*"

"I came to the conclusion it would survive without me. You didn't bring that little *pisher* with you, did you?"

"No."

"Good. This would be wasted on him, along with table manners and the Queen's English." He placed a hand on Valentino's back and shoved him toward the open door. There was nothing wrong with the old pedant's stores of adrenaline.

The projection room looked like an ordinary college classroom, which it was much of the time, with rows of desks for film students to sit and watch movies and make notes. A stout projector stood on a table facing a collapsible screen. They crossed the room without stopping. Broadhead entered a code into a wall panel, opened a steel fire door on the buzzer, and held it for Valentino. A pneumatic tube pulled it shut behind them.

This was the room reserved for projecting cellulose nitrate, air-conditioned to an even seventy degrees year-round, and enclosed entirely with firewall, so that if the film caught fire, the blaze would destroy only the projectionist and his audience instead of spreading beyond the room. To slow down that process, heat-sensitive sprinklers pierced the ceiling and there was an extinguisher illuminated on every wall. The projector, a permanent fixture bolted to a steel stand, was several times larger than the one in the outer room, with oversize Mickey Mouse–ear magazines to contain the reels and seal them off from outside catalysts. It, too, was equipped with an air-cooling system capable of regulating the temperature in a building of modest size.

The facility had cost as much to install as a plush private theater with all the extravagant trimmings, but all the money had gone into technology and fire prevention. It was just big enough to throw a clear image on the flame-retardant screen, the palette was industrial beige, and folding metal chairs provided seating. Indirect lighting came from behind ceiling soffits, not to enhance mood, but to prevent the heat of the bulbs from coming into contact with the stock. It fell upon a flat can lying open and empty on the worktable beside the projector stand, like a clamshell that had given up its meat. Valentino picked up the lid, turned it over, and read the label. His heart bumped.

"You can project it?"

"*I* can, yes," Broadhead said. "The dues I pay to the projectionists' guild would keep me in mahogany, but it's a lot more convenient than digging up someone with a card on short notice, and most of them don't know the first thing about handling vintage. They might as well be twirling spaghetti."

"I meant the film."

"The stuff from the room next to the projection booth had me worried; conditions there were much less stable than the basement. Thank God we're in a desert. When I saw there was no rust ring on the cans, I began to hope. I spent four hours last night with a techie in the lab, opening reel one, here, and unrolling it inch by inch. There was no adhesion, and only the odd amber spot."

"Smell?"

"Like film. *Old* film — this isn't science fiction — but not like vinegar."

"Stage one?"

"Very early. More and more I think the old stuff's reputation is undeserved. They've dug it out of landfills after ninety years with the footage on the outside of the reels shot to hell but the inside ready to show to the public. I'd like to see safety stock make that claim. I'll crawl out on an academic limb and predict the basement reels are in as good a shape or better."

Valentino hesitated, half afraid to ask the question. "Is it *Greed*?"

Broadhead winked. "Possess thy soul in patience, my son. Lights!" He flipped the switch on the projector with a flourish. The screen glowed.

Valentino hastened to switch off the lights and sat down in the nearest chair. He watched the old familiar countdown, the numerals and characters jumping a little because of broken sprocket holes, from ten to one with a nearly unbearable mixture of anticipation and impatience laced with apprehension; it wouldn't be out of character for his friend and tormentor to work him up to a fever pitch only to bring him crashing down with a Three Stooges short borrowed from the part of the archives that was available to every freshman.

The first image demolished that fear — and held him in thrall until the end of the reel. It was the golden-tinted Art Deco emblem, with reclining lion and sconces, announcing "A Metro Goldwyn Picture," from that brief moment in time before Louis B. Mayer had added his name to the company that began with the merger of his studio with Samuel Goldwyn's while *Greed* was in production. The sound era would replace the static image with an actual lion, turning its head toward the audience and roaring defiance at competitors and all other forms of entertainment. Many of the happiest hours in Valentino's life had started with a glimpse of that noble beast, its maned visage encircled by a banner with the company motto: ARS GRATIA ARTIS ("Art for Art's Sake"). Next came "Louis B. Mayer presents an Erich von Stroheim Production"; then, in great black capitals outlined in yellow upon a field of gold nuggets sinisterly sparkling:

GREED

He applauded explosively. He couldn't help himself. A glance back over his shoulder revealed Broadhead's round rumpled face set in a mask of supreme self-satisfaction, a clump of hair fallen over one eye, his unlit pipe in his mouth in the light escaping through the louvers in the projector. The professor never sat down while showing a film, but stood in a wrestler's crouch for hours at a time, muscles tensed, ready to shut down the power the instant the machinery faltered; one jammed frame was all it took to start a fire.

Valentino had seen the picture before, in both the 133-minute truncated version released in 1925 and the four-hour restoration produced by Rick Schmidlin in 2000, using hundreds of stills and dialogue cards to provide some semblance of the original narrative; Valentino and Broadhead had contributed many of the photographs, acquired from estate auctions, overlooked library files, and junk shops whose owners had no idea of their significance. Von Stroheim's own continuity script, found among his effects after his death in 1957, had been used to interpret their meaning and establish their order. But the result, for Valentino at least, had been a disappointment.

It was neither von Stroheim's fault nor Schmidlin's, nor that of anyone else involved at either end. The photographic team of Ben F. Reynolds and William H. Daniels was superb, the San Francisco and Death Valley locations were vivid, and the performances of leading players Zasu Pitts and

Gibson Gowland reached beyond the screen and across eight decades to wrench the most jaded modern heart. It was a meticulous and sensitive reconstruction. But movies were meant to move. Nearly two hours of period snapshots inserted in long sections among the surviving action footage, with title cards to explain and connect, did less to reveal genius than it did to reduce the director's version to a stultifying evening spent in front of an undiverting historical documentary on PBS.

But *this* movie deleted every pixel of that unsatisfactory experience from his memory.

Based on Frank Norris' turn-of-the-century novel *McTeague,* the film lingered over every line and nuance of the book to trace the descent of a dim-witted but good-natured brute into resentment, obsession, and double murder. Fallen upon hard times after marrying the woman of his dreams, the loutish dentist is at first elated by his bride's lottery windfall, then puzzled by her miserly refusal to spend a penny of it to improve their lot. As bafflement deteriorates into rage, the sin of avarice turns deadly on several levels, dooming husband, wife, and best friend and ending in an irony as bleak as the desert where it takes place.

The first reel, of course, didn't go that far,

or even very far past the first plot point: the hulking dentist yielding to temptation and stealing a kiss from his pretty patient as she lies sedated in his chair — definitely an *ick* moment for moviegoers of the 1920s as well as today's, but presented with a subtle compassion that encouraged pity rather than revulsion. Von Stroheim's glacial pace, with slow camera pans and long close-ups of twitching faces, promised to take as much of his viewers' time as if they had sat down and read the book from beginning to end. Everything about the approach was alien, yet hypnotic, like watching a rather shabby flower opening its petals in stop-motion. It gave the subject beauty.

The tailpiece flapped through the gate, the screen went blank. Valentino was still staring at it, transfixed by the ghosts that still inhabited it, when he realized Broadhead was talking. For a man who shared his protégé's love for moving pictures, the older man seemed physically incapable of allowing the fantasy to fade before he charged ahead with his observations and opinions.

". . . no reason to call Thalberg a philistine for crying editor," he was saying. "The crazy Austrian expected audiences to catch the first four hours early in the evening, break for dinner, then come back and watch the rest until the milkmen came out. They put in ten hours on the job six days a week, and they weren't about to spend all Saturday night watching other people get more and more miserable and then go to church a few hours later."

Valentino rubbed his eyes. "They might have. The thing is we'll never know. They hated the version MGM released, said it was sordid. But that was the studio's film, not his. If they had the chance to see this version, his career might have gone the right way."

"Some say it did. He held up production on *Merry Go Round* for days waiting for authentic Austrian Army underwear to arrive from Europe, and not a thread of it showed onscreen. By the time Gloria Swanson got him canned from *Queen Kelly,* he was already on his way out. If *Greed* were shown his way and made millions, he'd still have wound up playing Kraut heavies for lesser directors. Never underestimate the ability of a mad genius to crap himself in public."

"So we've done it. Found *Greed.*" Valentino leaned sideways in his chair, feeling charged with energy and drained of emotion at the same time. "What's next?"

Broadhead turned off the projector. The

fans circulating cool air inside spun to a halt. "First, we get as much of it transferred as we can before the cops raid the joint." He swung open the magazine and removed the full reel. "I gave the techie who helped me unwrap reel one a hundred bucks to print up reel two. I'd have gone in order, but then I wouldn't have been able to show you the beginning, and I know how you feel about coming in after the credits. By the way, you owe me a hundred dollars."

"Why me?"

"It's your property, Rockefeller. Before the Oracle is through with you, you're going to be hemorrhaging money like *Cleopatra*. You might as well get used to it now." He placed the reel in its can. "What did Anklemire say?"

Valentino had decided emphatically not to mention that Anklemire had suggested solving the case for the police; Broadhead's opinion of the man in Information Services was low enough as it was. "He said I should butter up Sergeant Clifford with a personal tour of our operation."

"Interesting. Who'd have thought the little troll could make so much sense?"

"He also said I should call her first instead of waiting for her to make the first move, as if I were courting her. I don't think his sensitivity training took."

"I didn't say he'd know *why* he made sense," Broadhead said. "He's a Neanderthal savant. All these new scientific weapons in the war on crime have turned the cop with the flattest feet on the beat into a techno-nerd. If she sees firsthand what we're trying to do, the expense involved, she might be sympathetic. And he's right about approaching her. If she has to come fetch what she wants, you'll have to dig yourself out of a hole just to bargain with her on level ground."

"In that case, we'd better get back." Valentino stood.

"Leave the 'we' to the little piggy. As soon as I get this back in cold storage, I'm going home to sleep. I haven't pulled an all-nighter since Orson Welles kept me up drinking Paul Maisson and kvetching about what RKO did to *The Magnificent Ambersons.*"

Broadhead was gray with exhaustion. Valentino asked if he could get home all right.

"I drive better when I'm asleep. If you don't stop mothering me, I'll call Immigration on your construction crew."

"Thanks, Kyle."

"Oh. Call Fanta and bring her up to

speed. Her number's in my Rolodex."

When Valentino returned to his office, Ruth flagged him down with a fistful of telephone messages. Three of them were from Sergeant Clifford.

CHAPTER 8

He dumped the messages on his desk, slumped into his chair, and stirred the little scraps morosely with the eraser end of a pencil. They were written in Ruth's spiky hand on peach-colored sticky notes with a sun beaming in the corners; he figured the pad was a gift from someone who didn't know her very well and she was too thrifty to throw it out. Reporters had called from KLBA, the *Times,* the *Post,* and something called the *Prong.* Evidently the media had traced The Oracle to its new owner. He puzzled over a request for information from someone named Fresca until he realized it was actually Fanta who had called. Three others read simply, "Call Sgt. Clifford," with her number at the precinct.

He sighed. It wasn't the first time he'd let a movie get in the way of important business.

Still, he stalled; there seemed no reason

not to now. He got Ruth on the intercom. "What on earth is the *Prong*?"

"He said it was the student organ at Berkeley." She sounded even flintier over the speaker than she did in person. "I didn't like the way he said 'organ.' He sounded like one of those rappers. They say 'yo' a lot, like pirates."

"I thought the *Barb* was the student paper there."

"That's what I thought. He said it was reactionary, so he started his own. What's this about the Oracle and a skeleton?"

He filled her in, and closed his eyes awaiting the reaction. This was almost as bad as the chewout he had coming from Clifford. But Ruth surprised him.

"Beautiful theater," she said. "My first husband proposed to me there while Errol Flynn was wooing Olivia de Havilland in *Captain Blood.* It was a revival," she added, "on a double bill with *The Sea Hawk.* I'm not as old as some people seem to think."

"Maybe I'll run them both again in your honor when I reopen. I may need the income to handle the mortgage."

"I wonder if that skeleton was there that night."

"I doubt it. If the police expert was right, it was placed there long after the house stopped showing big-ticket films." He hesitated; an opinion was something one never sought from Ruth. She gave them out like gum. "Was I mistaken to buy it?"

"Someone had to. I'm glad it was you. The last thing this town needs is another gym."

He thanked her, hung up, drummed his fingers on the desk, lifted the receiver from his telephone, and dialed.

"I was about to send a squad car," Clifford said when he'd identified himself. "I talked to Anita Sarawak this morning."

"Anita who?"

"Your realtor. She said there were a lot of film cans in the room by the projection booth when she showed you the place yesterday morning. We found only a few when we went through it. They were empty."

Valentino said nothing, avoiding a trap. He'd had experience with reluctant informants, old-time film people's personal servants and the like, and knew the power of silence. Some people would say anything to fill it.

"Our CSI team found steel shavings on that empty shelf in the basement that match the ones I had a couple of uniforms bring back from upstairs. I'm asking you again what you took away from my crime scene."

"*Is* it a crime scene?"

"It is until I say it isn't. If I have to ask the question a third time, it'll be downtown."

He took a deep breath and told her about *Greed.* He'd barely begun to explain the circumstances of its filming when she interrupted. "I'll send someone to pick it up. You'll get a receipt, and you can reclaim it when my investigation is finished. You might have to wait longer if there's anyone alive to bring to trial."

"It's a priceless historical artifact. It needs to be stored in a stable environment." He made his lecture on the fragility of silver nitrate brief. "Sergeant, why don't you come down and visit our facility? I think you'll find it instructive from a professional —"

"How long does it take to knock off a copy on this safety film?"

"In this case, a month at least, working in shifts. It has to be done a frame at a time, and the length of —"

"You've got three days."

"How do you know the film has anything to do with that skeleton?"

"How do you know it doesn't? It's two minutes past ten. If it isn't in this precinct by three minutes past ten Friday morning, I'm sending that squad car: for you *and Greed.*"

He'd just hung up on the dial tone when Ruth buzzed him on the intercom. "You've got a call on line one. That Sergeant Clifford."

"I just spoke to her."

"She says she forgot something."

Instructing him to punch line one was unnecessary. His department seldom received enough calls to activate the second line. He pushed the button and picked up. He had the childish hope she'd changed her mind.

She started talking before he could say hello. "Ever hear of a director named Castle?"

He ran a thumb through his mental file. "William Castle. He shot horror flicks on the cheap during the fifties and sixties. He used gimmicks to amp up the reaction: battery-charged seats during *The Tingler* to shock the audience, painted sheets on wires to send spooks flying over their heads during *Thirteen Ghosts.* Sometimes he hired actors to run up and down the aisles in hideous costumes. Early experimental theater."

"That checks. Department computer shows him answering a public-nuisance complaint in nineteen fifty-eight for scaring an old lady half to death during a showing of something called *The House on Haunted*

Hill, at the Oracle. Care to hear the particulars?"

He said yes. He felt a tingle, as if he were sitting in one of Bill Castle's electrified seats.

"Seems a wire or something broke thirty minutes in and a certain object dropped into the old lady's lap. She wet her pants and hollered cop. Guess what it was."

"A human skeleton."

"Maybe you've got a little detective in you after all. Well, this Castle is a skeleton himself now, so we can't interview him. But if no dental records turn up suggesting otherwise, which is a crapshoot anyway after all this time, we may safely consider Mr. Bones an alumnus of some medical-school anatomy class and redirect our energies toward murders that took place in this century."

"Then you won't need the film."

"We've got three days minus ten minutes to establish that. You're on the clock."

"What does Harriet Johansen say?"

"About what, the case or your perfect cheekbones? I'm not a dating service."

"She said I have perfect cheekbones?"

"DNA's no good without a national database or a surviving relative to provide a match. That brings us back to finding the dentist who put in those fillings forty or fifty

111

years ago, and since this one isn't exactly a department priority, you're going to surrender those reels before we turn up any X-rays."

"What's the hurry, if it's not a priority?"

"Because I had to come to you. If you'd given up the information yesterday, I might have been in a mood to work something out."

"I was in shock, Sergeant." He almost added, *and under peer pressure,* but there was nothing to be gained by ratting out Kyle and Fanta. "I can have two reels for you by Friday, and the rest as they're transferred. Please? I'm sorry, sorry, sorry."

The line was silent. He was beginning to think she'd hung up when she came back on. "The answer's no. But I *will* take you up on your invitation."

"Invitation?"

"To tour your facility. Maybe it'll give me an angle on this case I hadn't considered."

That was encouraging. With Kyle along, wearing the charm he assumed for cocktail party fund-raisers, he thought he might be able to bring the Big Red Dog to heel. "When would you like to come down?"

"Not me. Criminalist Johansen. You two seem to speak the same language. Wait for her call."

This time the connection broke. He sat chewing the inside of a cheek. He thought of calling Broadhead for advice, but he decided not to disturb him; he was worried about the old fellow's health after twenty-four hours without sleep. He picked up the phone to call Anklemire, then put it down without dialing; twenty minutes with that little fugitive from the Warner Brothers animation department were exhausting enough. Then his gaze fell to one of the message slips on his desk.

He got up suddenly and charged across the hall. Ruth glanced up from her computer. "What's the matter, on the lam?"

"I left something in Dr. Broadhead's office."

"Hope it's still there. He never locks the door. Someday he'll find his computer missing."

"It's a Wang."

He didn't need the computer. Broadhead only used the huge museum piece to write letters to colleagues, which he printed out and sent by snail mail. Valentino, who had carried in Fanta's message even though it contained nothing useful, spun the Rolodex on the desk, found her number, and called her from Broadhead's phone.

"Oh, hi," she said. "Well, is it the real deal

or is it the bogus hocus-pocus?"

He heard plumbers working in the background, complete with banging wrenches and cursing. When the volume went down suddenly he realized she'd been listening to music.

"It's the real deal, but I can tell you all about it later. What do you know about William Castle?"

"The hamburger tycoon?"

"That's White Castle. Never mind, I'll handle that end myself. How's your course load?"

"Not bad today. I've got archery practice in an hour."

"Can you blow it off?"

"I — don't know. . . ." She drew it out, sounding guarded.

It struck him then he was talking to an attractive coed who was probably hit on often. He hastened to tell her about Sergeant Clifford's demand.

Her tone changed. "That's a bummer. The way Dr. Broadhead explained it, you can't copy anywhere near eight hours of film in that time."

"Or ten. Turning over the original isn't an option. I could go to jail, be a hero, but it wouldn't save *Greed*. She'd just get a court order and seize the reels."

"Bummer to the twelfth power. I didn't mean to get you in trouble."

"I'm a grown-up. That means I can get in trouble all by myself. Anyway, it was the right thing to do. When a man is murdered, that's one man's tragedy, but a work of art belongs to all of us."

"What can we do?"

He felt himself smiling. "I'm glad you said 'we.'" He told her.

"Wow?"

" 'Wow?' Isn't there some New Age expression that fits?"

"Not for *Greed.* Um, and 'New Age' is kind of old maid."

Valentino scratched his neck, checking for wattles.

"Will Dr. Broadhead be joining us?" she asked.

"He's resting. He was up all night working in the lab."

"Is he okay? I mean, that can't be healthy for a man his — in his position."

"Now you sound like our secretary. She thinks the world would be a better place if everyone acted his age." But he was touched by the young woman's concern. Broadhead could lecture for hours on the inattention and ingratitude of the current crop of undergraduates.

"I talked to her on the phone this morning. What's her problem?"

"You're young. She's not. But she knows everyone in the industry. So what do you think?"

"This is my first murder," she said. "Where do we start?"

CHAPTER 9

They divvied up two of the four estates. Fanta took Government, Valentino the Press.

Dropping her off at the Civic Center, he watched her cross the sidewalk, a tall, slender, self-assured young woman in a white linen jacket and khaki slacks, cork-heeled sandals on her tanned feet. She'd tied her blue-black hair in a ponytail and put a notebook and pen in a leather shoulder bag. He'd noticed during the drive that she'd pruned the kid stuff from her speech. First impressions counted. The Los Angeles County property records were open to the public, but it was possible to get a clerk with an attitude.

From there, Valentino went to the downtown branch of the library, where most of the staff knew him by name and greeted him with smiles and nods and here and there a tightening of nostrils, bracing for a request that would send them to the remote dusty stacks for an item no one had checked out in decades. He thought he heard a collective release of breath as he passed the desk and went straight to the microfilm reading room.

There among his most devoted friends — spools of film in boxes arranged by date and the Moviola-like readers in their carrells — he began scrolling through ancient numbers of the *L.A. Times* and the late great *Mirror.* After a while he stopped mooning over the advertised premieres of motion pictures that no longer existed and directed his attention to the local news. The readers were time machines, and there were occasions when he wished he could crawl inside one, reverse the crank, and travel backward with the pages preserved on film, wonderful film. Rumors that the library was preparing to transfer its newspaper files onto digital discs, for viewing on computer monitors, depressed him as nothing had since colorization.

Four hours later, woozy and shielding his eyes from the glare of the twenty-first century, he found Fanta in the place they'd arranged to meet, a microbrewery off the old Plaza where he and Kyle liked to hang out. The walls were plastered with four-sheets of W. C. Fields playing poker, Douglas Fairbanks in tights, and Marilyn fluttering too close to the flame. Reese Witherspoon and Johnny Depp had been added to attract a younger crowd, but the clientele so far had remained relentlessly middle-aged. Fanta and the wait-staff were the youngest people present.

At the moment, however, she looked older. She had unaccustomed circles under her eyes and smelled faintly of old plat books. She ordered a glass of stout.

"Can I see ID?" The waitress wore a ring in her nose and a James Dean T-shirt.

"Diet Pepsi." Fanta shrugged at Valentino. "Can't blame a girl for trying."

"Nothing to eat?" he asked.

"Now that you mention it, I've had a humongous craving for White Castle all day. I'll have the Scarface," she told the waitress. "Extra heavy on the blood 'n' gore."

Valentino discovered that she'd ordered a half-pound burger with double everything. The menu had changed since his last visit. "I'll have the clam chowder."

"One Buster Keaton." The waitress wrote on her pad. "Anything to drink?"

"Regular Pepsi."

"Have a beer," Fanta said. "At least I can smell it."

He ordered the stout, in her honor. Ordinarily he preferred something domestic and lighter in body. When they were alone, Fanta leaned her forearms on the table. "The Oracle changed hands three times between nineteen twenty-nine, when Max Fink sold it, and nineteen thirty-seven. The last time was to a guy named —"

"Warren Pegler," he finished. "He sold it in fifty-six to a film society. They showed Bergman and Fellini to college students, and broadened the program a few years later to include more popular fare. That was the generation that made stars all over again out of Humphrey Bogart and the Marx Brothers."

"Then mine came along and plunged them back into obscurity."

"I wasn't going to say that."

"It's true, though. Maybe my kids will reverse the cycle."

He smiled. "You have a fine vocabulary. You should use it more often."

"Totally. Only for right now I'd rather be a closet nerd. You know, we wasted a bundle of time if all we did was dupe each other's efforts."

"Your sources were more official. Newspapers were no more reliable then than they are now, especially the feature items. According to the *Times* — it was the *Times Mirror* then, before the takeover was complete — the society struggled ahead for several years trying to make ends meet, then gave it up as an expensive hobby and sold it to my realty firm, which rented it to a hippie commune until it could find a buyer. That turned out to be me, long after the hippies packed up their lava lamps and left."

"I got as far as the realtor," she said. "County records aren't long on colorful details, and they don't have you on the books yet."

"The world is waiting to see if my check bounces. The *Mirror* did a human-interest piece on Pegler when he took over. He was a double amputee, lost both legs in an accident in the developing lab at Metro-Goldwyn-Mayer, where he worked a dozen years earlier."

The food and drinks arrived. Fanta waited impatiently while the waitress set everything out, asked if they needed anything else, and left without waiting for an answer. Then Fanta pounced. "MGM did *Greed,* right?"

He nodded. "It's a coincidence worth looking into, but it's not remarkable when you know L.A.'s history. It's still a factory town, the factories being the studios, but it was even more so from the twenties through the forties. They were the biggest employers around, and MGM was bigger than all the rest of them put together. It's like trying to connect a Chevrolet assembly worker to something that happened at General Motors world headquarters."

"An assembly worker who bought himself a dealership," she said. "Where'd he get the bucks?"

"Metro's lawyers gave him a fat settlement to avoid a lawsuit. After he paid his hospital expenses he had enough left over to buy a block of shares in Warner Brothers just before *The Jazz Singer.*" He paused. "You know the story behind *The Jazz Singer*?"

"Al Jolson talks and sings, the box office lights up like Grand Theft Auto." She rolled her eyes. "Four-point-oh, film studies, Kyle Broadhead, Ph.D., hello."

"Sorry. Habit." He stirred his soup. "Long story short, he pulled out of the stock market two months ahead of the crash in nineteen twenty-nine. Eight years into a major depression, he still had the price of a lucrative theater franchise in his pocket."

"Your reading was way better than mine." She sneezed.

"Bless you."

"Thanks. They should dust that place every hundred years." She picked up her burger. "That reminds me. Did you call that Harriet person yet?"

He swallowed some chowder. He couldn't recall mentioning Ms. Johansen's impending visit to UCLA. "Call?"

"You thirtysomethings are worse than we are in the slacking department. There were so many sparks flying around that basement I was glad we got the film out of it."

"We exchanged polite words."

"Any more polite and you'd've finished up in the sack."

"At your age, maybe. I'm too young for 'Do your own thing' and too old for 'Whatever.' She sneezed and I said, 'Bless you.' I just blessed you when you sneezed. I didn't see any sparks."

"You didn't bless me the way you blessed her."

"Let's change the subject."

"Whatever. This Scarface burger is awesome. Al Pacino should work at White Castle."

"Maybe Paul Muni made it."

"Who?"

"The original *Scar*— oh, forget it. I am a geek." He pushed away his Buster Keaton, an experience less memorable than its namesake. "You did all right today. Not many athletes would skip practice to spend the afternoon in the cellar of the county building."

"Dibs on the newspaper files next time."

"Do you mean that?"

She met his gaze, then put down her sandwich and wiped her mouth and her hands. "Give me your best shot. What do you need?"

"A more specific time line, to start. Architecture and dental science puts that corpse in the basement room long after Fink, and common sense says it was before the realty firm took possession. It had to have been bricked in by then or someone would have found it. That's still a fifteen-year chunk. I need to narrow it down."

"It might be longer than that. Your realtor overlooked twenty-four reels of *Greed* upstairs."

"The saleswoman said there used to be a wall in front of it. They tore it down only recently. My guess is some flunky saw a lot of film cans, nothing unusual to show up next to a projection booth, opened a few, found them empty, and didn't bother to look any farther. Ignoring the human skeleton in the basement is something else altogether."

"I wonder why the reels were split up."

"Not important to the central issue.

Whose skeleton was it, and who bricked it up?"

"The murderer. Or an accomplice."

"If it was murder. Sergeant Clifford says the skeleton might have been a stunt to spice up a B horror movie." He told her about William Castle. "If her hunch pays off, the case is no longer official business, and we get to keep the film."

"Yes!"

"Except playing the hunch means eliminating every missing-persons complaint filed over fifteen years, until a trick skeleton is the only explanation left. Meanwhile *Greed* rots away in a stuffy room at the Hall of Justice."

"Oh."

"Hold on, there may be a shortcut. Someone disappeared late in the Pegler era or when the film society owned the theater. I'm assuming someone missed him and reported it to the police."

"That'd be in their files. Clifford must be all over it."

"Let's hope she hits the jackpot. I found some promising candidates in the old papers, but most of them turned up alive or dead in the later editions. I'm leaving the rest to the sergeant to run down."

"What's left?"

"I told you all I could find in four hours. You can skip past that, take my place in the reading room, and expand the search beyond L.A. Maybe someone with a connection to the Oracle went missing out of town and it wasn't reported locally. Check the suburban papers and the AP wire. I'd do it myself, but I have fences to mend." He avoided bringing up the Johansen tour for fear of reviving that conversation. He felt a flash of guilt. "It means missing classes. It isn't as if you could look up the subject in an index and go right to it."

"Yes, it is. It's called Google. I'll fire up the Mac and do a mouse hunt."

He laughed and sat back. "From the mouth of Generation *Y*. It never occurred to me to tweak the Net."

"While I'm at it, I can try to find what became of Warren Pegler."

"Burial or cremation would be my guess. He was thirty-one in nineteen thirty-seven."

"Maybe there's a daughter or a grandson. No legs doesn't mean no —"

"Romance. Knock yourself out. And Fanta? Thanks."

"Anything for the program. I might learn something I can use in my practice. Oh! I almost forgot."

They were seated in a booth, with Mar-

126

lene Dietrich looking at them down the length of her elegant nose. Fanta opened her shoulder bag on the seat beside her and took out something large and flat in a slick plastic bag. "I was early, so I killed a few minutes in Barnes and Noble on the way here. I hope you don't have it."

He took it and slid out a coffee table book in a varnished jacket. Grauman's Chinese Theater blazed in barbaric splendor on the cover in full color. The title was *Pleasure Domes: The Golden Age of the Picture Show.*

"I don't," he said, "but I can't accept it. I don't want to get in the way of paying off your student loans."

"It was remaindered. And I'm here on an athletic scholarship. I'm a very good archer. Turn to page ninety-four."

It was a two-page spread, of The Oracle's auditorium, taken at the peak of its grandeur. He ran his fingertips over the glossy surface. He could almost feel the contours in the gilded baroque ornaments and the deep plush on the seats. The photographer must have chosen a premiere night, and stationed himself in an upper balcony to capture the entire scene: Iconic stars and pioneer producers in dinner jackets and ball gowns shared the orchestra, chatting and holding programs. Every seat was filled.

Valentino's throat tightened. It was like looking at a snapshot of his mother in the full beauty of her youth. He made a mental note to call her.

"It's wonderful. Thank you." The words seemed inadequate.

"I just wish it were in color," she said. "What was it with black-and-white, anyway?"

"Everything's better in black-and-white. I think even Sergeant Clifford would bear me out on that."

CHAPTER 10

After he let Fanta out in front of her house, he used his cell to ask Ruth if Harriet Johansen had called.

"No, but everyone else has." She mentioned KBLA, the *Times,* the *Post,* and added the Associated Press to the list; it appeared the story of the corpse at The Oracle contained all the elements necessary to capture the attention of the national media. "That *Prong* creature called again," she said. "He's an insistent little punk. I bet he walks around with a boom box and a pistol."

"I'm sorry for the bother. It doesn't have anything to do with the office." Which wasn't really a lie, since none of the reporters knew what else the basement had contained.

"Don't apologize. This is the first time this department has justified the cost of installing telephone equipment. I haven't answered this many calls since the old days at

Columbia."

"Did Harry Cohn chase you around his casting couch?"

"Wouldn't you like to know."

He'd caught her in a playful mood, which was an event rare enough to encourage him to pursue the conversation.

"Some good may come of this," he said. "If I knew it would take a criminal investigation to draw attention to the program, I'd have stashed a corpse somewhere myself."

She shut him down. "Are you coming back? It's quieter than usual here with Dr. Broadhead gone."

"Later. I've got an errand." He reached out and laid a hand on *Pleasure Domes,* reassuring himself of the book's presence. "If Ms. Johansen calls, give her my cell number." He flipped the phone shut before she could pour another bucket of water into the tide of opinion about his love life. Was he so much the monk that a few pleasantries with an attractive woman should drench him in innuendo?

The likely answer was yes. He was a young man, reasonably good-looking if the old-fashioned matinee-idol type didn't produce snickers, and a healthy heterosexual. But he lived his work. Since that work involved countless hours spent chasing down scraps of celluloid in attics and whatnot shops, examining individual frames against the light, and wearing holes in the metal seats of the folding chairs in the UCLA projection room watching mute melodramas without even the enhancement of the original musical scores, his life must be charitably described as less than well-rounded. At times his own past experiences came back to him in a series of frames. He became corporeally insignificant the instant he stepped outside the shot.

"My God," he said aloud. "I'm Norma Desmond."

It was a subject that needed serious consideration before he entered a lonely middle age filled with the empty clutter of pop memorabilia and framed certificates of merit awarded by obscure fellowships dedicated to arcane cinema; but not today. Not this moment. He had an overpowering urge to revisit The Oracle — *his* Oracle — and run his hands over the fossils and pottery shards of Old Hollywood.

The building, conceived upon a Jew's idea of a cathedral, but scaled down to nestle into the relatively horizontal cityscape of Tinseltown in the 1920s, assumed a tombstone aspect under the low smutty skies of

Los Angeles post-1960. The uniformed officer standing sentry at the entrance represented a later model of Valentino's nemesis in the parking garage. He compared the visitor's features with the picture on his driver's license, spoke into the two-way radio clipped to an epaulet, and got an answer crackling back.

"You can go in," he said. "Don't touch anything."

Valentino ducked under the yellow police tape stretched across the doorway and entered the lobby. He had it to himself just then, but could hear sounds of activity beneath his feet, where investigators would be moving crates and dismantling racks in the basement, searching for bullets buried in the walls or whatever. He felt a sense of violation and trespass — and at that moment assumed in full the role of property owner, with all its challenges and responsibility.

The room was cavernous, a colossal waste of space by Eastern standards, and completely in character with the idolatry of excess that had dictated fashion in the age of sheiks and shebas, Theda Bara's milk baths, and champagne fountains at Pickfair. Its designers had striven to shame the pharaohs of Egypt, but they had neglected to build in the permanence of the Old Kingdom. The workmen were the same who had erected the Tower of Babel for *Intolerance* and the Roman Coliseum for *Ben-Hur;* great edifices made of plywood and papier-mâché, intended to stand throughout principal photography, then to be knocked down or left to decay in the Hollywood Hills. Without regular maintenance, mildew and tarnish and termites moved in to claim their inheritance. A pane had fallen from the smiling countenance of the archangel in a stained-glass window, making him look as if he were missing a tooth.

Just because he could, and to declare defiance of officer's orders, Valentino drew a furrow with a finger through the chalky dust on the glass surface of the candy counter, then tugged the sheet off a hunchback shape beside the staircase to the mezzanine. A cloud erupted. He stepped back to avoid being enveloped, but it left a fine skin of dessicated architecture on his shoes. He regarded the plaster cast of Pegasus with nostrils distended, wings poised to unfurl, one forefoot raised for takeoff. The gilding had flaked off the Grecian curls on the equine forehead, leaving the impression of balding, and a careless mover or a kid with an air rifle had knocked a huge chip out of a knee, but Valentino thought the sculpture could be restored. Its mate was another story. The pedestal that had supported it on the other side of the staircase was vacant. It would have to be replaced, and he had serious doubts about finding a capable craftsman or the money to compensate him. It would be more practical to remove the remaining figure.

A terrible chilling sensation of buyer's remorse racked him. The theater was too big, too far gone, there was too much to be done, and he didn't know where to start. And *Pleasure Domes* had described The Oracle as one of the smaller surviving picture palaces!

He sneezed. How Freudian, as if he could expel the burden through his nose.

"Bless you."

Startled, he looked up at the creature descending the stairs. The naked bulb someone had wired in place of the chandelier cast a halo around short blonde hair, and for a nanosecond he thought a stained-glass angel had separated itself from a window to rescue him. But she was wearing Harriet Johansen's smock and carrying her tackle box. He noticed her legs were well shaped, with trim ankles and long graceful muscles in the calves.

"Thank you," he said. "I thought you were finished here."

"I wanted another look upstairs, for signs the victim was killed there and moved to the basement. Post-mortem lividity's not an option when there's no flesh on the corpse."

"What did you find?"

"Some interesting stains. I did a hemoglobin test on what looked like a classic arterial-laceration pattern — slit throat — but it looks like someone just got careless opening a can of soda. Old semen traces in the projection booth; quite a lot of semen. I prescribe Clorox and plenty of it."

"Free love," he said. "This was a shrine to the Age of Aquarius for a while. Before my time." He felt foolish adding it.

"That explains the traces of cannabis I found in a floor crack." She stepped off the bottom stair and shook his hand. Hers was cool.

"You carry equipment to test for marijuana?"

"Everywhere I go." She touched her nose. "Don't tell the boys in the narc squad."

"Sergeant Clifford thinks the skeleton might have been left over from a horror-show spectacle back in the fifties. It might have come from a medical school."

"She told me. I had to disappoint her.

Skeletons used for demonstration purposes are linked together with wire, to keep them from falling apart when you tap them with a pointer. That had never been done with this one. There would be wear marks and traces of metal. Also I scraped skin cells off the floor where the body was found. It did all its decomposing here on the premises." She read his expression. "I'm sorry. I'm sure you're anxious to start renovating."

He was grateful that Clifford hadn't been generous with the information about *Greed.* He preferred to choose the time and circumstances of the announcement. "It isn't your fault. Have you figured out what killed him?"

"The skull was fractured, glancing blow from a blunt instrument. It might not have been fatal if he'd received medical treatment. As it was he probably lapsed into a coma and died either from starvation or shock."

"Shock, I hope," he said, with a shiver. "I never got over *The Black Cat.* I saw it on WGN when I was eight and I never had the courage to watch it again."

"That's a brave admission to make to a stranger. Most guys try to macho it out."

Great. He was coming off as a wimp. "What else have you found out?"

Her face lapsed into deep thought, which in her case was deep indeed; she struck him as fiercely intelligent, even beyond the demands of her work. Then she shrugged, with a bright toss of her head that sent electricity tingling to his nerve ends.

"I suppose it will be on tonight's news," she said. "The last satellite truck pulled out only a few minutes ago; the crew got tired of waiting for the criminal to return to the scene of the crime after fifty years. He was in his late teens or early twenties, slight of build, probably not too well off. Those fillings in his teeth were primitive work, possibly by a student at a college clinic. Middle European, based on the cranium and mandibula. German or Dutch would be my guess. Don't quote me on that. Profiling's verboten. I don't want to be picketed by boys in Buster Brown haircuts and wooden shoes."

"I thought all that CSI mumbo-jumbo was Hollywood hogwash."

"There's a healthy dose of science fiction on those shows, but nothing we won't have in a few years. A lot of money goes into criminology research, thanks to the statistics. We don't have the authority those actors have. We can't carry guns, for instance, or interview suspects, or threaten them with arrest. Those specialties belong to people like Karen Clifford."

"Her name's Karen? I didn't know that."

She smiled, with a narrowing of her exotic eyes. "What's *my* first name?"

"Harriet." He felt himself blushing.

"You have the advantage."

"I only use mine at the DMV and to get airline tickets. My friends call me Val."

"Is that an invitation?"

"Yes." He answered without hesitation.

"Don't call me Harry. People in this town make assumptions based on your haircut and your line of work."

"I like your haircut. It fits the shape of your skull."

She smiled again, and this time she released the full candlepower. "Val, you couldn't have made a better choice of words with a forensic pathologist."

"I wasn't thinking," he said. "This is a euphemistic minefield, isn't it?"

"I'm not offended. Ghouls rule. You're in the industry, right? You must have to deal with your own share of BS. Convenience store clerks pushing screenplays."

"I'm not with the industry. Most of my clients are as dead as yours. I'm an archivist with the UCLA Department of Film Preservation." He braced for the reaction.

"I *love* old movies. Astaire and Rogers."

"Laurel and Hardy."

"William Powell and Myrna Loy."

"Joseph and Herman Mankiewicz."

Her face clouded. His stomach sank.

"That's where people start to make assumptions," he said.

She tossed her head again. He could get used to that. "I'd like a tour sometime. It's a wonderful building. You don't see a lot of lath-and-plaster these days. Every cent I make seems to go into my rent, and I can hear my neighbors brushing their teeth."

It made him think of *The Crowd.* He shoved that aside like a Trekkie hiding the Klingon dictionary in his closet. "How about right now?"

"I have an autopsy at two. A drowning, three days washing around in the surf off Malibu. Black tie only. That means gas mask and neoprene. Rain check?"

"Speaking of a tour —" He was reminded suddenly of more pressing things.

"UCLA film lab. Sergeant Clifford told me. How's tomorrow morning?"

"Nine o'clock?"

"It's a date."

She left swinging her instrument case, sensible heels snapping on a floor paved with priceless marble and cheap linoleum and dust. Distractedly, he patted the balding head of winged Pegasus and pushed his way through the marvelous swinging inlaid mahogany-and-ebony door into the auditorium.

Erich von Stroheim greeted him, a ghastly figure separated in shreds and tatters from what remained of The Oracle's linen screen, hanging like silk stockings from the rail at the top of the stage. He wore a cutaway coat with tails, a stiff shirtboard, and a black-rimmed monocle attached by a ribbon to his lapel: the butler in *Sunset Boulevard*, reduced by devotion and circumstances from Norma Desmond's first director (and first husband).

"You are a handy fellow with the ladies, Herr Valentino," he said. "But how are you at saving *mein Kindling?* I see no progress."

Valentino blinked. He was wide awake now, he knew it; yet he was facing a ghost. He'd made the mad leap from harmless obsessive to full-blown psychotic with no stops along the way. Best to humor the vision; and by reflection himself.

"I've taken steps," he said. "Reel two's in process of transference to safety stock. I had to screen reel one to be sure we had what we thought."

"But you allow yourself to be distracted.

Die Frauen — *Ja,* they provide comfort in times of trouble and help to propagate the species — but also they distract us from the business at hand. You must focus. This is a metaphor, *ja?* And yet it was so important to art — *mein* art — that the world embraced it as a model to emulate. Emulate, this is the right word, *ja?*"

"*Ja,*" Valentino said. "I mean yes. But you're overlooking an important issue. You're dead. You've been dead for forty-eight years. I have a hard time accepting advice from a corpse."

"And yet who else has such wisdom of experience?" No humor showed on that stern face, separated as it was into disconnected pieces, an eye here, half a nose there, the mouth twitching out of line with the other features, like a reflection in a shattered mirror. "Seek the dead for your counsel, Herr Valentino. They have all the answers."

And then he was alone.

The ribbons of torn fabric hung blank from the frame, stirring slightly in the current of air coming through broken slates on the roof and places where joints failed to join.

" 'Seek the dead for your counsel,' " Valentino muttered. "Can't you spooks talk any plainer than that?"

For reply, The Oracle groaned on its foundation.

CHAPTER 11

"You need to have new cards made." Kyle Broadhead ran a pipe cleaner through the barrel of his pipe. "You've got *detective* on the brain."

The professor looked as much like an unmade bed as ever, but the linen appeared fresh. He'd regenerated himself completely from the exhausted wreck of yesterday morning. Valentino wished he could say the same for himself. He'd had a rocky night after his phantom encounter; needing rest and yet reluctant to lapse into unconsciousness for fear of inviting the apparition back. He'd fallen asleep finally without dreaming, but any resemblance he bore to a fully functioning human being came from the jumbo Starbucks cup perched on the corner of Broadhead's desk.

"I don't see any other approach," Valentino said. "Clifford won't back off from her ultimatum. We have to crack the case to save

Greed."

"And what can you bring to it that the entire Los Angeles Police Department can't?"

"Passion and determination. It's just routine for them, apart from the snazzy trappings. Without a weeping widow or some other cause celebre to fan the fire, the press will lose interest, and failing that there's no pressure to solve it. But you and I and film history will never recover from the loss."

"Who's responsible for this sleuthing bug, you or Henry Anklemire?"

"I admit he's the one who brought it up, but he was thinking of the publicity. All I'm interested in is preservation."

Broadhead ran thick fingers through his rumpled hair. "I wish you'd run all this past me before involving Fanta. The police are treating it as a homicide, after all. You're perilously close to child endangerment."

"She's past the age of consent. And anyone with a personal interest in keeping the case unsolved would be too feeble by now to put up much of a threat. If it's murder, chances are the murderer is dead. You're going to have to come up with a better reason than that to let the matter drop."

"How about getting in the *real* detectives'

way, bollixing up *their* investigation, and ensuring the worst possible scenario?"

"It's just old records, Kyle. Public property. It's not like we're scaring off eyewitnesses."

"Well, you know where I stand. Saving a film and solving a murder is a pip of a double feature to try to pull off. You're a scholar, not Sherlock Holmes. While you're galumphing about sniffing for clues, some illiterate housemaid in Pasadena could be snipping up *The Wind* to start a fire in the hearth."

"It isn't fall yet. I think we can wait till New Year's to worry about that, when the thermometer drops below seventy."

"That isn't the point and you know it."

Valentino gulped coffee. "I'm not as far out of my element as you think. In our work we need many of the same skills as a professional investigator: interviewing people, combing through dusty files, playing hunches, making connections. A scrap of celluloid can wriggle itself into a much smaller hole than a murderer."

"And a country deacon can run for pope. But he isn't likely to get very far with the college of cardinals." He rammed the pipe cleaner through one last time. The inside of the barrel must have been as clean as a dairy by then.

"This is getting us nowhere. Did you talk to Coppola about speaking at commencement?"

"This morning. He's going to be shooting in Germany then, but he agreed to a satellite feed. It took some persuading. I had to remind him who got James Wong Howe to see him when he was setting up American Zoetrope. Our president's making arrangements to bring giant TV screens into the auditorium, like you see at Rolling Stones concerts. And he's greenlighted *Greed.* It still won't be finished in two days and counting. I couldn't get him to commit enough techies to set up an assembly line on one project. There's a lot of inventory, and each item is someone's foster child."

Kindling, Valentino thought. He took another hit from his cup. "I wouldn't be too hard on him. He's not a film person."

"Most people aren't, and I include the industry. It's all about the Deal; but then it always was. Otherwise every scrap of footage ever shot in this town and on location would be safe on shelves, and I'd be teaching freshman English to troglodytes. God only knows what *you'd* be doing, a dreamer like you."

"Tour guide at the Hollywood Wax Museum," he said. "Which reminds me. I'm showing Harriet Johansen through the lab in half an hour."

Broadhead's smile was sly. "Anklemire suggested Sergeant Clifford."

He didn't rise to the bait. "Clifford suggested Ms. Johansen. A gathering of nerds, as it were. Join us? I never saw a skinflint you couldn't charm out of his checkbook."

"Not this time. This time I'd just be in the way. You've got Cupid in your corner."

"I've had just about enough of that. This isn't junior high."

"Don't be offended when I say I don't care if you ever find the love of your life. She's attracted to you: Clifford saw it, Fanta saw it, and so did I. You'd be a blind fool not to use it to buy time."

"That's cold-blooded."

"No more so than butting into an official investigation. It's all about saving *Greed.*"

"I'm thinking of taping that to my bathroom mirror. I ran into Johansen in the theater last night." He told him what she'd said about the skeleton.

"I could have told you it wasn't the one Bill Castle used. He kept it hanging in his study among all the other knickknacks from his pictures. Forrest J. Ackerman, the publisher of *Famous Monsters of Filmland,* bought it from his estate. He dresses it in a tuxedo at Halloween."

"I didn't want to disturb you," Valentino said. "No danger of you picking up that habit." He watched Broadhead put away his pipe and drop the cleaner into his wastebasket. The basket was empty otherwise. His was the least cluttered environment Valentino had ever seen, inside and outside academia. His house was the same way; he could clean it with a leaf blower. No telling how many valuable posters, playbills, and props from movie sets he'd given away or dumped. The movies themselves were all he cared about.

"What were you doing at the theater, hanging curtains or playing Bulldog Drummond?"

"No. I was trying to measure the full extent of what I'm getting myself into."

"I'll get you Leo Kalishnikov's number," Broadhead said. "He designs high-end home theaters for movie stars and industrialists with the cash to spend. Nothing on your scale as yet, but he has a real affection for the old barns, and he uses better material than Loew's or Paramount."

"Can I afford him?"

"*That* feature's gone into general release. But you're going to have a nice piece of change coming when you sell *Greed* to the university."

"I'm not doing this for profit. I'm donating it."

"Don't be a sentimental blockhead. If this august institution can shell out a hundred thousand to put Francis Ford Coppola on closed-circuit from Berlin, it can pay you fifty for the distribution rights. That's just a little over a grand a reel. It's worth much more, but you can assuage your bruised conscience by offering it at a discount. Take the money and run. But stop when you get to your office. I can't carry the weight of this program on my shoulders."

"Is that a confession or a compliment?"

"It's a statement of fact." Broadhead rocked back and forth in his swivel. "So what's the condition of your investment? I wasn't concentrating so much on the building as on its contents when I visited."

"I think it's structurally sound. Better than I am," he added, on a sudden impulse. He'd intended to remain silent on more disturbing recent occurrences.

"I thought you looked frazzled. I put it down to White Elephant Syndrome. I had it myself thirty years ago, when I signed my mortgage agreement. I expect to lose it when I make the final payment next month."

He decided to make a clean breast of things. Who could you tell you thought you were going crazy, if not your best friend?

"The good news is the Oracle isn't haunted by the ghost of Max Fink. The bad news is Erich von Stroheim's moved in." He described his dream of two nights before and the hallucination in the theater last night.

"The uniform he was wearing the first time," Broadhead said when he'd finished. "Was it the one he wore in *Foolish Wives* or *The Merry Widow*?"

"*Foolish Wives.* I always thought he looked like a Shriner in *Widow.*" He wondered where this was heading. The other asked the oddest questions at the oddest times.

"The old screwball loved to play dress-up. He claimed to have been a member of the imperial court. I don't think he ever forgave his father for being a Jewish hatmaker in Vienna. He tacked the *von* onto his name when he emigrated."

"I forgot to ask him about that." Valentino waited.

"The butler's livery last night was an encouraging sign. He's getting less formal around you. That means he doesn't feel he has to make as big an impression."

"Are you humoring me?"

"No. Remember, it's your delusion, not his. If you're getting more comfortable with him, maybe it means you're coming to terms with your decision to buy the Oracle."

"I didn't know you had psychiatric training."

"Where we live, formal training would be redundant. It's in the air. Half of Southern California spends half its time on the other half's couch. We could apply for a degree on the basis of simple osmosis."

"Am I nuts?"

Broadhead chuckled. "By local standards you don't even qualify for eccentric. If I shared the details of all the recurring dreams I had in that six-by-eight cell on the Yugoslavian Riviera, I'd be weaving baskets in Camarillo."

"But I wasn't asleep the second time. There's a name for people who see and hear impossible things when they're wide awake: lunatics."

"How do you know you weren't asleep?"

"Because only horses sleep standing up."

"Did you ever sleepwalk when you were a boy?"

"Never."

"You probably had one of those revoltingly happy childhoods one hears so much about these days. Let's take inventory of what's happened to you in the last forty-eight hours." He tapped his desk, one finger at a time. "You hurled yourself without warning into a lifetime of debt, made the discovery of your career, found a corpse in your basement, and committed yourself to race the largest and best-equipped police force in the state to the solution to that mystery. What else? Oh, right. You fell in love."

"I did *not* —"

"Okay, began an infatuation. You have to meet me halfway if we're going to cure your condition. Any one of those events is potentially life-changing and cause for stress. If you weren't experiencing some form of disturbance, I'd diagnose you as catatonic."

"You're not just saying that?"

"Val, have you ever known me to just say anything?"

" 'Seek the dead for your counsel.' What do you think that meant?"

"Sounds like good advice. Isn't that what we do all the time on this hallowed ground?"

Ruth buzzed him on his intercom to announce that a Miss Johannesburg was there to see Valentino.

"I wish she weren't too vain to wear a hearing aid," Broadhead said.

"I think it's misogyny. Yesterday she called

Fanta Fresca." Valentino stood. "So you think last night was just my subconscious trying to steer me in the right direction?"

"Well, there's another explanation."

"What?"

"You see dead people."

CHAPTER 12

Outside the shapeless smock, Harriet Johansen had a trim waist and handsome upper-body development in a knitted top and pressed blue jeans, her slim ankles on display above two-tone leather flats. Valentino thought it was a shame her work required her to cover up and wear a mask.

The air around Ruth's desk simmered; she regarded every attractive female below the age of fifty as a threat to her position.

Ms. Johansen, who was either impervious to the vibrations or unaware of them, smiled in relief when she saw him, wearing a lightweight sport coat over an open-necked shirt and slacks. "I had second thoughts on the way over," she said. "I wondered if I should have dressed for the lab."

"I didn't invite you here to put you to work." He shook her cool hand. Ruth's computer mouse clattered like a tommy gun.

They took the stairs. In the echoing well, the criminalist asked if something was wrong with his assistant.

"Ruth," he said after a brief confusion. "She doesn't answer to that title. She's the last secretary on the Coast. She's also a walking overloaded circuit. You never know when she's going to short out."

"I know a lieutenant who's the same way. He should have been chief of detectives years ago, but he always figures out a way to cheese off the brass around promotion time. It's going to be a lot more quiet downtown when he retires."

"It'd take a charge of dynamite to retire Ruth. She laid the rails that brought the first carload of movie people to this town."

Yesterday's smog was yesterday's smog. Once outside, she fished a trim pair of sunglasses out of a woven-leather purse and put them on. He said, "You'll have to fight off the paparazzi if you wear those off campus. You look like Meg Ryan's daughter."

"Kid sister. But thank you." She slid them down Lolita-style, watching him. "You don't look that much like him."

"Like who?"

"You know who. I was engaged to a negative cutter at Sony. We went to Toronto once, to take in the film festival. They were screening some early Rudolph Valentino shorts they found in Canada, from before *The Four Horsemen of the Apocalypse.* I thought he looked like a cross-dressing woman. Was he gay?"

"There's been debate. After he put on that beauty mark in *Monsieur Beaucaire,* he spent the rest of his life trying to prove he wasn't a pink powder puff." He hesitated; should he brag? "I had a small hand in bringing those early two-reelers to the surface. An anonymous bidder bought them in a lot at Pola Negri's estate auction. I finally tracked him down in Ontario."

"Why didn't you bring them back to UCLA?"

"The Canadian government filed an injunction against the U.S. State Department, declaring them national treasures that couldn't be removed from the country. They'd still be in storage while the bureaucrats battled it out, but I had a friend in Montreal who offered to donate some rare Alaskan gold rush documentary footage to the Smithsonian. The State Department backed off. It was a sweetheart deal: The documentary stuff had greater historical value, and now anyone who wants to make the trip can enjoy both."

"Your friend just decided to donate?"

"Well, we discussed it."

"Doesn't sound like such a small hand to me."

"It was, though. Preserving and restoring film is as much a team effort as making one. What you're about to see is only part of the process." He glanced at her. "You're the first person who's heard of Rudolph Valentino who didn't think I look like him."

"You're the first person who thought I looked like Meg Ryan's daughter."

They entered the preservation building, where a red bulb in a steel cage was flashing above the door to the laboratory.

"We can't go in now," he said. "It's crunch time on a major project, and a stray hair or a speck of dust could ruin a morning's work. But we can watch the show."

He led the way to the thick window that looked into the room. The technicians were in full battle dress, masks and safety glasses and shiny black gloves, smocks to their knees, paper slippers covering their shoes. They were washing forceps and scissors in the stainless steel developing sinks, adjusting the thermostat on the storage cabinet, turning the crank on the mammoth copy camera. Light flooded the room evenly and everything looked as clean as in an incubator.

"If I didn't know better, I'd swear I was still downtown," Harriet Johansen said. "What's everyone doing?"

"They spend most of their time cleaning their instruments. A piece of grit you can barely see can make a scratch twenty feet long onscreen. That fellow there has the crucial responsibility of making sure the temperature in that storage cabinet never exceeds seventy degrees and that the relative humidity stays below fifty percent. To heat and moisture, celluloid is like sugar to an ant. The cabinet's built to hold a hundred and fifty thousand feet of film. It's strictly short term, for work in progress. After that it goes into the vault downstairs for extended storage. You can guess what the camera's for. Transferring silver nitrate to safety stock is a frame-by-frame process. A lot of people think it's just a matter of pushing a button, like copying videotape."

"Why isn't it?"

"For the same reason you don't unwrap a three thousand-year-old mummy by yanking on the bandage. This is brittle stuff in the first stage of decomposition."

"No wonder they have to wear so much gear."

"That's for their protection, not the film's. In the second and third stage, it releases nitric and nitrogen dioxide, among other nasty gases. Extremely toxic. When it reaches stage three, it goes in there." He pointed at a schoolbus-yellow cylinder standing three feet tall in the center of the room, with a lock-lid on top and a scarlet skull-and-crossbones on the side. Stenciled warnings in three languages appeared below.

"I guessed it was fragile. I never knew it was dangerous."

"That's just the tip of the iceberg. After stage three, it goes into a steel drum and the drum goes to the bottom of the Pacific, next to all the nuclear waste. That's if it doesn't burn or blow up en route."

She smiled. "Now you're exaggerating."

"Only a little, because every precaution is taken to prevent combustion. The material's laced with silver. Silver oxidizes, oxidation produces heat, and celluloid is extremely inflammable even in its pristine state. If it were introduced today, the Federal Trade Commission would never allow it to go on the market."

"How many stages of decomposition *are* there?"

"Five."

"*Five?* Three sounded scary enough. What

happens in stage four?"

"It degenerates into a glutinous mass, fused into an orange lump that smells like vinegar. In the final stage it crumbles into a fine powder that's about as volatile as magnesium. You know, photographer's flash powder. Poof!" He sprang open his hands.

She tilted her head toward the technicians. "Are they in danger?"

"Minimally. They're trained to handle hazardous materials. We installed ventilation fans and an automatic sprinkler system in compliance with OSHA and the National Fire Protection Association and made some improvements of our own. People who specialize in removing asbestos are at greater risk." He had a sudden premonition of personal crisis.

She saw it on his face. "You're thinking about the Oracle, aren't you? Old theaters and asbestos go together like fried potatoes and grease."

"There's a lot of insulation hanging out of the ceiling," he said. "But Max Fink was cutting corners, trying to save money. Maybe he used rock wool."

"We'll keep a good thought." She touched his arm. Then she turned back toward the window. "What is safety stock?"

"Cellulose triacetate. Kodak brought it

out in nineteen forty-eight, and within three years it replaced silver nitrate at all the studios. It met all the performance requirements and was fire retardant besides. The jury's still out on whether triacetate adds much to the actual life of the film. The hues of Technicolor seem to resist fading in the old stuff better than the new. We'll know more when it's been around as long as what came before. Bored yet?" He smiled. He could still feel the touch of her hand on his arm.

"Not at all. So the one with the copy camera is striking off a new print on triacetate from silver nitrate. What's the film? You said it's a major project."

"A wonderful old silent that's been missing for eighty years."

"What's it called? Maybe I've heard of it."

He knew the subject would come up, but he decided it was too early to hit her up for a word on behalf of his mission. "*Greed,* directed by Erich von Stroheim."

She popped her head in that little shrugging movement he liked. "I score okay on some of the highlights: *Citizen Kane* and William Randolph Hearst, the Gish sisters, John Ford's westerns. I know Marcello Mastroianni isn't a kind of pasta. Douglas was the buff."

"Douglas was your fiancé?"

"Yes. The first time I called him Doug, he corrected me. I should have known where it was going then." She looked troubled. "I'm picturing Erich von Stroheim, why is that? Directors are kind of invisible."

"You probably saw him in *Sunset Boulevard,* his swan song. He couldn't stay away from the other side of the camera. He played Gloria Swanson's butler."

"Yep. Saw it. Can you *show* silver nitrate?"

"Only as late as the first stage, and then it requires a special projector with an air-cooling system. It's an experience no one should miss. The silver provides an illumination all its own; a glossy glow that's lost in transference to triacetate. When they called it the silver screen, they weren't just being poetic."

"If you're asking me to the movies, I accept."

She kept her profile turned toward him, watching the technicians at work. He said, "I'll set it up."

" 'Flammable Solid,' " she read from the English legend on the side of the drum; back to business. "What's the difference between 'flammable' and 'inflammable?' "

"There isn't any. Too many people were smoking around oil tankers, thinking

162

'inflammable' meant 'uninflammable.' It was cheaper to change all the signs than educate them."

"Like 'irregardless.' "

"Exactly. Only in this case people were blowing themselves up."

He spoke of molecular sieves and ester-base film, formaldehyde and sulfur dioxide, pointed out the air-quality monitors, and was about to suggest a visit to the storage facility in the basement when the technicians started climbing out of their protective gear. The red bulb above the door had stopped flashing. He looked at his watch.

"That's lunch. My God, I've been jabbering for two hours." Way to make an impression on a first date.

"Are you serious? It seemed like five minutes."

They entered the lab, where he introduced her to the crew, one of whom was a woman a little older than Ms. Johansen. "Marge is our safety inspector," Valentino said. "If we get any more shorthanded, we're going to have to get the head of the department down here to help empty the wastebaskets."

Marge, a short redhead with freckles the size of dimes, gripped the visitor's hand tightly, one woman in a male-dominated trade to another. "We should get together sometime and swap war stories," she said. "How'd they break you in?"

"My section chief made a sandwich out of a human liver and slipped it into my sack lunch. What about you?"

"Someone poured vinegar in my locker; I never found out who. I was on my way to the dump barrel with my favorite cashmere sweater when the laughing started. So did you take a bite?"

"Just a nibble."

One of the others showed her a section of negative on safety stock. Valentino couldn't resist looking over her shoulder when the man held it up to the light. It was the seduction scene in the dentist's office. Harriet Johansen asked if it was a stag film.

"It was a little less scandalous in nineteen twenty-five," Valentino said. "They told rape jokes back then. We're going to take some heat from several special-interest groups when this is released. One of the secondary characters is bound to attract the attention of the Jewish Anti-Defamation League. Luckily for us, von Stroheim was a Jew."

"And Stepin Fetchit was black. That didn't stop the NAACP from hounding him to his grave." Marge laughed. "If you hang around with these characters long enough, you'll qualify for a film-school diploma."

Harriet said, "I've learned plenty just this morning. I'm looking forward to walking Val through the county morgue."

"Val, is it?" The technician, a rawboned post-graduate named Artie, grinned. He'd joined the preservation program on the advice of Kyle Broadhead, who'd smashed his hopes for a directing career with a failing grade. "We were told to expect an official visit."

Valentino decided to stop that conversation in its tracks. "It is official. California's a first-name-only state. I guess they didn't teach you that in North Dakota."

"South Dakota," Artie corrected.

"What part?" Harriet asked.

"Rapid City."

She uncased that brilliant smile. "I'm from Pierre."

"We beat the pants off you on the varsity court."

"We got them back on the football field."

Valentino and Harriet left. In the hallway, he asked if she was free for lunch.

"My father used to say, 'Free, white, and twenty-one'; but I don't want to offend any special-interest groups. I've been starving for an hour, ever since I mentioned fried potatoes. Is there a good place close by? I should get back, but no one downtown

165

knows how long it takes to tour a film preservation laboratory."

They took his car to the Sunset-Vine Tower and got a table in Room at the Top, just ahead of the rush. Their window spot looked out on a hundred years of Hollywood history. The waitress, an obvious would-be starlet in makeup too heavy for her tender years, brought them a salad and a breast of chicken. Harriet stuck a fork into her romaine. "How'd you get interested in movies?"

"I've taken up enough of your time on that subject," he said. "What drew you into criminology?"

"My father was chief of police in Pierre. I guess it's in my blood. I enrolled in the program at USC on the theory that the practical experience in Los Angeles has it all over the smash-and-grab specialists in South Dakota. I guess that doesn't make me any less of a starry-eyed kid than our waitress."

"I saw that too, but you're no starry-eyed kid. You got a spot on the LAPD."

"Well, they need women who can make the grade, to wheadle budget allocations from the politicians. We're not nearly as well represented as we are on those TV shows. But how many male viewers are going to tune in to watch some stud shaking a test tube?"

"False modesty's almost as bad as idle boasting. I saw you at work. Sergeant Clifford doesn't strike me as the type who defers to just anyone."

"I've worked with her a couple of times. If she doesn't make lieutenant on the next round, I may just join NOW. But we can discuss my work when it's my turn to conduct a tour." She munched on a radish. "First-date food orders don't count. Where do you stand on sushi?"

"Do you like it?"

"I'd rather eat my latex gloves."

"Thank God." He exhaled. "Vegetarian?"

"Douglas was, which made me one, too. The night we broke up I went to Ruth's Chris and ordered a porterhouse as big as my head."

He laughed. She watched him. "Are you seeing anyone?"

"Most of the women I meet started collecting social security before I was born. I almost popped the question once."

"May I ask what happened?"

"Religious differences. She was Three Stooges, I was the Ritz Brothers." He savored the sound of her laughter. It was deep and unguarded. "Dog person or cat fancier?"

"Dog," she said. "But I work too late to keep one. You?"

"Same story. I don't have a friend I'd trust to feed and walk it while I'm in Cannes. What do you do when you're not busy dissecting cadavers?"

"I run, when I'm not at work and the smog won't defeat the purpose."

"Me, too. Everyone out here's into good health habits, and the air's more poisonous than —"

"Stage-five silver nitrate," she finished. "We should run together sometime, when our schedules are both in line and the air's clear."

"I don't like those odds."

"Then we'll bring our masks and pare them down." She swallowed a piece of lettuce, then drank Perrier. Their eyes met above the candle flickering in its orange holder. "A glass of Chardonnay would make this go down smoother," she said.

He smiled. "A bottle would be even better." He looked for their waitress.

CHAPTER 13

Valentino was sitting in the tumbledown clutter of his office, staring at the wall, when Kyle Broadhead came in without knocking. The professor made room for himself in a chair and played with his pipe. "What's the scoop?" he asked.

"We saw Quentin Tarantino. He was coming in as we were leaving, with an entourage bigger than the cast of his last movie. None of them had on a jacket. The headwaiter ran out of loaners and had to give Tarantino his. Since the waiter was built like Brian Dennehy, I'll bet he dragged the sleeves through every course."

"You took her to lunch?"

"We went Dutch."

"Tacky."

"She insisted. The dating scene's changed since your day."

"For the better, I think; at least until the IRS lets you write off a dinner disaster as a bad investment. Still, it's a good sign. You got along."

"She's smart and funny. Even the technical stuff held her interest."

"You didn't bore her with trivia, I hope."

"At lunch, she asked me about my interest in movies, but I changed the subject. You'd have been proud of me."

"I am proud of you. So is she going to plead our case with Sergeant Clifford?"

Valentino's heart took a dip. "I forgot to ask."

Broadhead stared, his hands frozen in the midst of twisting his pipe apart.

"I thought of it once, but the time didn't seem right. Then I never thought of it again. I'm sorry, Kyle. I screwed up."

He twisted it back together, dug out his pouch, and filled the bowl. His friend watched him strike a match and draw at the tobacco. He let a ball of blue smoke escape out the side of his mouth. "Congratulations." He shook out the match.

"Are you being sardonic? I can't always tell."

"I'm sincere. I've been worried about you lately, but I see now you're going to be all right."

"Worried about me how?"

"There were rumors."

"About what? My sexuality?"

"Your lack of it. Eighty years ago I'd have felt compelled to play the surrogate father and arrange an assignation for you in Tijuana. In those days, people didn't go down there for the designer knockoffs. Movies are escape, not life. You can't live it and hide from it at the same time."

"Movies are my work. Yours, too."

"You're half right. I watch them because I'm paid to, and then only to confirm I've found what I was looking for, or gather material to lecture to young imbeciles. When I want to relax, I'd rather listen to music — not a motion-picture soundtrack — or read a book — not a history of cinema. Not you. You eat, drink, and breathe the things, and now you've begun to dream them. You can't escape them even when you sleep. You've had it all backwards. But if you can worm your way into the confidence of a woman who's in a position to help you in your work and not even remember to take advantage of the situation, there's hope on the horizon."

"But what about *Greed*?"

"Civilization seems to have stumbled along without it all these years. If the film crumbles to dust in police custody, I suspect the species will survive." He leered around his pipe stem. "Anyway, who's going to search for the stuff that's still lost if the Valentinos of this world don't try to be fruitful and multiply?"

"Is that why you've been riding me about her for two days?"

"No. That was recreation. Are you going to see her again?"

"Are you asking that as a colleague, a friend, or my surrogate father?"

"A friend. We've established I don't care all that much for movies, and I have no connections in Tijuana."

"She offered to take me on a tour of the forensics lab at police headquarters."

Broadhead frowned. "Not promising."

"I invited her to the movies, sort of. I didn't know it was an invitation until she accepted."

"Better. Something with Julia Roberts, I hope."

"Zasu Pitts. I sort of talked myself into asking her to see a film printed on silver nitrate, for the experience. *Greed* seems appropriate, since that was what was being processed when I took her through the lab."

Broadhead rolled his eyes. Then he made a gesture of resignation with the pipe. "Baby steps are better than standing still."

"It also gives me another reason to help

the police close the case before they confiscate the film. It would be socially awkward to ask Harriet for any favors now."

"You're hopeless. If I cut your throat, you'd bleed movie popcorn butter." The professor rose, took a fold of paper from an inside pocket, and dropped it atop the heap on the desk. "That's the number I promised you, for the theater designer. Do your old friend a favor and call him right away. Construction's a bitch, but it keeps you too busy to meet with underworld characters in parking garages."

Left alone, Valentino remained quiet a moment, breathing secondhand smoke. Then he mouthed a silent apology to Broadhead and dialed Fanta's number first. It was busy. He hoped that meant she was making progress with her online investigation. Then he unfolded the scrap of paper and called the number written in Broadhead's neat block hand.

A youthful tenor with a light Russian accent answered. "Kalishnikov Imaging."

"Mr. Kalishnikov, please."

"Speaking."

Valentino introduced himself and explained his errand. He'd barely mentioned West Hollywood when he was interrupted.

"The Oracle," Kalishnikov said. "Wonderful! Every day I expect to pick up the *Times* and see it's been demolished. You know its history?"

"Quite a bit of it. I'm willing to bet you know more." He experienced a sudden surge of inspiration; perhaps the designer knew something that would help clear up the mystery. But the man on the other end dashed that hope by reciting a long list of the architectural influences that had gone into its construction. It was of no practical use unless the murderer were a citizen of Byzantium or old Granada.

Suddenly Kalishnikov interrupted himself. "Wait. The Oracle. I'm getting something."

Valentino waited. He felt as if he were having his fortune told.

"I *did* read about it in the *Times*," the designer said. "The crime section. Are you the one who found the skeleton?"

"Yes. I'm sorry if you find that up—"

"Terrific!" The implied *y* between the second *r* and the first *i* came straight from the Black Sea. "I love a project with a sinister past. Tell me truthfully; is it haunted?"

He hesitated. He wasn't at the point where he confided his ghostly visitations to strangers. "There's a legend, but what building in this city doesn't have one of those after fifty years? Poor old Max Fink."

"Who? Oh, yes, Fink. Tough break."

That laid to rest any hope of a solution from the Russian's corner. He'd know all there was to know about the architect, but nothing about the various owners. Valentino was about to ask what he charged for consultation when Kalishnikov spoke again.

"I must see it. When may I?"

"Whenever you like, if you don't mind ducking under police tape."

Kalishnikov asked him to hold. He came back on after a moment to announce that he was meeting with a building inspector in Beverly Hills tomorrow afternoon. Could Mr. Valentino meet him at the theater at three o'clock?

"Certainly. But it's not Mr. Val—"

"Terrific!" The line went dead.

He'd just cradled the receiver when the telephone rang. He snatched it up, hoping it was Fanta.

"You made an impression on my CSI," said Sergeant Clifford, without greeting. "Tell me you didn't promise to take her away from all this. She's the only one I can talk to without a medical dictionary in my hand."

He let that slide. "What progress have you made on the investigation?"

"We're pursuing several leads. She said she told you that was no trick skeleton you found. I'm going to need that film."

"This is Wednesday. You gave me till Friday morning."

"The William Castle stunt angle was looking good then. When it went blooey I Asked Jeeves about *Greed.* You didn't tell me collectors were offering up to half a million for a complete print."

"I didn't know that, though I'm not surprised. In my area you tend to think more in terms of artistic value than market price."

"You and I don't work the same area. When it comes to murder, I look for a motive, and the good old seven sins are always at the top of the chart."

"Greed." He couldn't resist.

But her mind was working more linearly; she didn't react. "Allowing for inflation, fifty years ago those reels had to have been worth ten or fifteen thousand. People have been killed for a whole lot less."

"But if stealing them were the motive, the murderer wouldn't have left them behind with the victim."

"Maybe he panicked. More likely he walled them up with Mr. Bones intending to come back for them later, when there was less chance of getting caught with them. When we know who was killed and who killed him, we'll know more of the circumstances. There's no chance of retrieving latent prints after all this time, but if there's a bloody thumbprint on one of those cans and we can trace it through the FBI data base, I can send the media wonks home and focus my attention on the killers that walk among us."

He saw his out. "You can have the cans any time. Standard procedure requires removing the reels from the original containers anyway and packing them in fresh aluminum or polypropylene."

"I don't care if you pack them in Cracker Jacks. I'm not Harriet Johansen. I'll send officers to collect those cans. If we don't turn anything there, we'll need to check the film itself for content."

"Content?"

"Two years ago, my lieutenant cracked the alibi in a domestic homicide when the suspect showed up in a crowd shot on KBLA. Since then we've maintained a cordial relationship with the tape librarians at all the local stations."

"If your suspect showed up in *Greed*, he's either dead or too old to stand trial."

"Well, we can't speculate on the connection until we've seen the show."

"It's archival material, Sergeant. You can't show it on any old projector."

"We pay people to sit in rooms and examine that kind of evidence by hand, frame by frame."

His chest felt constricted; he wondered if this was how it felt to go through cardiac arrest. "With all due respect, I can't allow a desk jockey downtown to handle eighty-year-old film over a box of Dunkin' Donuts!"

"I'm glad you said it with all due respect. Otherwise I'd be there in an hour with a court order, demanding immediate surrender of the evidence in question. It's two-fifteen. You've got less than forty-four hours."

He was getting used to sitting there holding a dead phone.

Ruth buzzed and told him she was putting through a call from "that *Prong* person." When he opened his mouth to protest, a stranger interrupted him.

"Claudel Blount, Berkeley *Prong*." The voice was deep but youthful, with a slight drawl. "You're the man who found the deceased?"

He reminded himself to ask Ruth to brush up on her diversity. This man was no rap-per. "Yes, but I —"

He had to put the man on hold to answer the other line. He recognized the light baritone of the evening anchor on KBLA. "Mr. Valentino, we've been trying to reach you for days. Would you agree to a live telephone interview about the Oracle Mystery?" His tone capitalized both words.

"I don't think the police would — hang on." The intercom was buzzing.

"The *Times*," she said. "On three."

"We have a three?" Before she could answer, he asked her to tell the caller he was out. Then he returned to Claudel Blount.

"I just wanted your comment on the fact that a busload of Native Americans here at Berkeley is on its way to Los Angeles to picket the theater," said the young man from the *Prong*.

"Whatever for?"

"Their spokesperson says they're concerned the remains may be tribal and will end up as an irreverent display in a museum."

"The bones aren't Indian!"

"Are you an anthropologist?"

"No, but —" He stopped himself before he could blurt out what Harriet had told him about the body's dental work and probable ethnic origins. He didn't want to get her in trouble by going public with details the police might be holding back, or anger Sergeant Clifford into revoking his grace period. "Talk to the police." He excused himself, cut the connection, and spoke to the TV reporter. "I just own the building. I'm a film archivist. I'll be happy to go on the air and talk about my work, but I don't know anything about murder."

"It *is* murder, then?" The mellow voice was deadly calm.

His heart bumped. That was a bad slip. "I can't answer that one way or the other. The police don't confide in me. If you want to ask me about film preservation —"

"Thanks for your time."

The intercom buzzed.

"I'm out, Ruth," he said. "Tell them I'm in Tibet, looking for the abominable snowman's wedding video."

She left the speaker on. "I'm sorry, Miss Shasta. He's out."

He'd cracked her code. He jammed his thumb down on the lighted button before Ruth could hang up. "Hi, Fanta. Sorry about that. I've been conducting an impromptu press conference."

"I'll call back."

"No!" He barked it. He apologized again.

"People have been hanging up on me all day. I'm starting to feel like a telemarketer. Did you turn up any unexplained disappearances around the time Warren Pegler sold the Oracle?"

"Sure, but I did better than that. I found Pegler."

"You're kidding. Alive and kicking?"

"Maybe, if he had legs. But alive for sure."

■ ■ ■ ■

III
DISH NIGHT

■ ■ ■ ■

CHAPTER 14

The printout was from the *Pittsburgh Dispatch,* dated Friday, November 30, 1956:

POLICE SEEK PHILANTHROPIST'S SON

Officers with the Missing Persons detail of the Pittsburgh Police Department are searching for the estranged son of a prominent contributor to local charities after the son failed to show up at his mother's home for a promised Thanksgiving visit Wednesday.

Albert Spinoza, 21, a former assistant projectionist at the Roxy Theater in Pittsburgh, left the home where he lived with his parents, Abraham and Eloise Spinoza, three years ago after an altercation and had not been heard from until last week, when he telephoned his mother to say he was returning for a visit, according to Mrs.

Spinoza, who was honored recently with a Citizen of the Year Award for her many large donations to nonprofit foundations in the area. She told officers that the death last December of her husband, Albert's father, had persuaded him to end their estrangement.

Mrs. Spinoza arrived at Union Station Wednesday morning to meet her son's train, but he was not aboard. A clerk with the railroad told the *Dispatch* that no record exists of anyone purchasing a ticket anywhere in the United States under the name Albert Spinoza.

Lieutenant Howard Prosper of the Missing Persons detail said that foul play is not suspected at this time. However, he said that because of Mrs. Spinoza's prominence in the community, every step is being taken to trace her son.

Valentino skimmed the sheet, then read it a second time more closely. He was seated in a blown-out upholstered armchair in the room Fanta shared with a female classmate, absent at the time. Precisely half the room was heaped with discarded clothing, stained pizza boxes, and college texts, while the other half — where Fanta sat in front of her computer — was as neat as if someone had dragged an enormous crumb scraper to the center of the floor. One bed was made, the other invisible under detritus. There was a dormitory smell of pepperoni and neglected laundry, and someone outside the open door to the hall was listening to Eminem.

"What nationality is Spinoza?" he asked.

"Dutch, I think."

"That's encouraging. Harriet Johansen said the victim was probably German or Dutch. The age is right."

"If you'd told me she said that, I might have had this yesterday."

"Forgive me; I've been preoccupied. How the heck did you find this?"

She smiled, all trace of resentment gone. Today she had on cutoff jeans, a denim baseball cap with her ponytail flowing out through the hole above the adjustable band, and a blue T-shirt that read LAWYERS DO IT ON THE BENCH. She was barefoot.

"I've got a Word Menu program on the computer. I had it keyword every job connected with a movie theater, on the hunch there was a professional link to the Oracle. I figured if it came up empty I'd just start from scratch. *Projectionist* hit the jackpot."

"Did you stop there?"

"Duh. No, and I forgive you again for asking. An usher went missing in St. Paul in nineteen sixty and a candy-counter clerk did a Winona Ryder from a theater in New Jersey with the night's receipts in fifty-four, but they found the usher drowned in the Mississippi a couple days later and arrested the clerk at a bus station. Anyway there were local connections in both cases."

"We still can't connect this one to the Oracle. I don't like the fact his parents seem to have been well-to-do. Harriet said who-ever drilled and filled Mr. Bones's teeth did it on the cheap."

"So it's Harriet now." She grinned.

He sighed. "Yes, Fanta, it's Harriet. I'm carrying her love child."

"Whoa!"

He apologized yet again. He seemed to have developed a habit of it with her. "I didn't get much sleep last night."

"I thought you looked bummed. Spinoza ran away, don't forget. Even if they wanted to give him his allowance, they wouldn't have known where to send it. Maybe he couldn't stay away from the Milk Duds in the lobby and went to a quack." She pointed at the printout. "The *Dispatch* ran a follow-up a week later, when the cops called off the search: no leads. I can make you a hard copy of that too, but it was mostly rehash."

He shook his head. "This would explain why there was nothing in the L.A. papers. If the Pittsburgh police made inquiries there, it wouldn't have been considered news. I doubt Spinoza's own hometown sheet would've covered it if his mother weren't a local hero."

"If there was an inquiry, wouldn't it be on file with the LAPD?"

"The big-city departments were just introducing computers then; dinosaurs with cooling units that filled rooms. If they bothered to transfer it to the memory bank back then, they wouldn't waste space on their current hard drive with an obsolete file on a routine request from clear across the country."

"Then Sergeant Clifford won't have this."

"Not unless she did what you did." He flicked the printout with his hand. "As good citizens, we're obliged to report this."

"Morally, yeah. Legally —"

"— it isn't evidence. That was your argument last time, and look at all the trouble it caused. The sooner she has this information, the sooner the case gets wrapped up and we get to keep *Greed.*"

"Unless it's a wild goose chase, and she wastes a lot of time the film doesn't have running it out." She turned her chair, a vinyl swivel patched all over with duct tape, tore a sheet off a pad on the computer station, and turned back. "This is where we'll find Warren Pegler. We can ask him about Spinoza and save the cops some shoe leather."

He read the hastily penciled note, recognizing the name of the Motion Picture Country Home in Woodland Hills. As a former studio technician during the Golden Age, Pegler would qualify for residency. "You just typed in his name and out came his address?"

"If it were that easy, you *would* have had this yesterday. But the older you get, the wider the paper trail."

"He must be a hundred."

"Ninety-eight. I pulled up his birth record. He's a native, born in San Diego under Teddy Roosevelt. Married and widowed, no children. I found that feature piece you mentioned from when he bought the Oracle, but no documents or ink to back up the claim he lost both legs in an accident at MGM."

"Hospitals move, their records get lost or go into the incinerator when they collect enough dust. Since the studio settled out of court, it probably kept the story from the papers at the time. After the Taylor and Arbuckle scandals, the last thing the industry needed was another, and back then it had the clout to silence the local press."

"I was with you right up until Taylor and Arbuckle."

"Not important. They were too hot to handle in nineteen twenty-two, but now they're as cold as Albert Spinoza, if that's him down at the morgue." He took out his cell and punched buttons. "I've got a friend in Admissions at the Country Home. She can tell me if Pegler's in shape to receive visitors."

"You memorized the number?"

"Most of my sources have lived there for years. One or two more trips and I can claim it as my voting address." A receptionist answered. "Kym Trujillo, please," he said.

"Valentino!" This was a husky female voice, lightly touched by a Hispanic accent. "You ready to check in? You could hold your own in the conversation in the cafeteria."

"Ask me again next year. I'd like to arrange a visit with one of your residents. Warren Pegler."

"I know Warren. I admitted him myself. He's a quiet sort, very popular with this crowd. Hang on."

He waited three minutes. A picture of the late U.S. Supreme Court Chief Justice William Rehnquist and a James Dean poster hung on Fanta's side of the room, opposite a painting of a bloated dead horse on her roommate's.

Kym came back on, sounding subdued. "I talked to one of his nurses. He's an Alzheimer's case, has his good days and his bad. Today's not so good. He's usually at his best in the morning."

He thanked her and said he'd call back then.

"I overheard," Fanta said. "How many girlfriends do you have?"

He decided not to get mad. "She's too valuable a contact to risk getting personal with." He folded the printout, put it in a pocket, and patted it. "A possible victim and a possible witness — or suspect," he said. "Two for one. Dish night."

"What's that?"

"During the Depression, theaters gave away a free piece of china with each ticket, one night a week. The idea was to keep customers coming back to collect the set."

She shook her head. "I'll never take it all in. This is worse than studying for the bar."

"You're doing fine." He struggled out of the quagmire of his chair. "That was excellent work. You'll make a great lawyer."

"That sounds like the dump speech. I'm

going with you tomorrow, aren't I?"

"How many classes did you miss while you were sitting at that computer?"

"When I want to be hassled I'll call my father. I'm the one who *found* Pegler."

"If you went up there with me, all you'd be doing is reading magazines in the visitors' room. I earn my salary talking to these people. They're old and frail, their memories come and go, they know their weaknesses and they intimidate easily. Whatever Pegler's part in this is, he might think he's being ganged up on by two strangers. If he panics or clams up, we'll have made the trip for nothing."

She slumped forward, resting her wrists on her bare muscular thighs. "My nana was in a nursing home, with dementia. She got violent sometimes, and she was the sweetest old gal you ever met."

"She was the script girl?"

She nodded, staring at the floor.

"It isn't the dump speech," he said. "If anything comes of this, I promise you'll be the first one I call."

"Hey!" She sat up. "What about getting to see the show?"

"The show?"

"Hello?"

He was tireder than he'd thought. "I've

only seen the first reel myself. It might be on safety by now. Dr. Broadhead will have to screen it anyway, to make sure it came out all right. You might have to watch it in negative," he said. "At the pace they're going, they can't stop to strike off a positive print."

"Insider stuff. Cool." She put on flip-flops.

He called Broadhead's line. Ruth answered. "Hang on, he just got off the phone. That Yolanda woman tried to reach you."

It took him a second to make that leap. "Johansen. She's a forensic scientist, not a stripper. Did she leave a message?"

"Something about owing you a tour. I'm putting you through now."

Broadhead listened to Valentino, then said, "Reel one came out of the soup this morning. It needs to dry twenty-four hours. I can run the original, if you don't mind sitting through it again. I assume you want to be present for the unveiling."

"You assume right."

"You two still playing Nick and Nora?"

"I'll tell you about it when I see you." He flipped the phone shut, yawning bitterly.

"Why don't I borrow my roommate's car and drive myself?" Fanta asked. "You should go home and crash."

"Not on your life. Turns out you're going

194

to see it on the original silver nitrate. I want to witness the reaction. Anyway, if I went home I'd just lie there trying to stay awake." He told her about von Stroheim's ghost. He'd been stonewalling so much lately it felt good to trust someone with an embarrassing confession.

"Cool," she said when he finished. "Ectoplasm."

"Dementia. Maybe when I'm at the Country Home I should pick out a room."

"I agree with Dr. Broadhead. Maybe you're not hallucinating."

"You've been watching too many Wes Craven movies."

"It's a haunted town, I've known that my whole life. We've got dead people's footprints in front of Grauman's Chinese, streets named after dead directors, dead stars in the homes on the maps to the stars' homes. My folks took me to the Alamo once on vacation. When I walked in, I felt the same thing I feel when I walk on Sunset, only there it's Davy Crockett and here it's Steve McQueen."

"Most people don't get advice from Davy Crockett and Steve McQueen. Why should I be singled out?"

"Let's look at it from the spook's point of view. The old bugger was pretty bummed out about what happened to *Greed,* right?"

" 'No matter if I could talk to you three weeks steadily could I possibly describe even to a small degree the heartache I suffered through the mutilation of my sincere work.' He said that to his biographer. I memorized it."

She nodded. "I think that's why he singled you out."

CHAPTER 15

"Well, if it ain't the Great Lover."

Valentino frowned at the attendant in the campus garage. "That was John Gilbert."

"I bet he never forgot his pass."

"Parking fuzz," said Fanta as they drove past the raised gate. "Probably came out here looking for a part on *Hill Street Blues*."

"*Dragnet,* more likely. I've looked high and low for that damn pass."

"Maybe von Stroheim took it."

On the landing outside the hall to his office, Fanta laced an arm through one of his. "Let's give Ruth a case of the fantods."

His judgment was too foggy to protest. As they strolled through the door arm in arm, Harriet Johansen turned their way from the desk.

She wore a light summer dress that clung to her in all the best places. The orange spark in her eye when she saw him and the young woman quickened his heart and stopped it at the same time. Behind the desk, Ruth took in the scene with an expression distilled from satisfaction and disgust.

Instinctively the newcomers parted. Valentino stepped forward. "Harriet, you remember Fanta."

"It's a little different meeting you outside a crime scene." The CSI's voice was toneless.

"Hi. I wouldn't have recognized you without your smock."

"I wasn't expecting you," Valentino said.

Ruth snorted and rattled her keyboard.

"I came to take you up on that movie invitation," Harriet said. "Afterward I thought I'd walk you through the lab downtown."

"Your timing's perfect. Dr. Broadhead and I were about to screen *Greed* for Fanta. That's the major project you saw us working on yesterday." He was talking fast.

"Another time." Harriet looked at her watch. "I just remembered I'm supposed to assist with an autopsy." She went toward the stairs, heels snapping on the linoleum.

"Can I call you downtown later?"

The door swung shut behind her.

Kyle Broadhead came out of his office. "I thought I heard voices. Let's get moving. We've only got the inner screening room till five." He stopped in mid-stride, looked from one face to the other. "Who died?"

"Some dude on an autopsy table," Fanta said.

Valentino's message light was blinking when he got back to his apartment. He and Harriet had exchanged home numbers. He pounced on it, but the message was from Ruth, reporting that a Mr. Khruschev had called the office to say he'd be a half hour late for their appointment at The Oracle. That would be Leo Kalishnikov, the theater designer. Valentino tried calling Harriet and gave up after eight rings.

The situation called for anxiety or rueful amusement, but by then he was too exhausted to feel anything but numb. He'd actually fallen asleep during *Greed*, and had missed experiencing that first reel all over again through Fanta's eyes. Her own expressed reaction, after Broadhead shook him awake, had seemed subdued. She hadn't been able to stop apologizing for the prank that had blown up in their faces.

But he was too far gone for mulling over the events of another roller-coaster day, and fell asleep seconds after slipping into bed. Von Stroheim, that master of irony and pity, chose not to disturb him.

He awoke refreshed, took a sip of instant coffee, and tried Harriet again. This time a machine answered; either she was screening her calls or had left early for work. He left a stumbling message of apology and explanation and asked her to call back. Next he got Kym Trujillo on the line.

"Warren's having a great day," she said. "He's on his way with an attendant to visit his wife's plot in Westwood Village Memorial. He always comes back in a chipper mood."

"It doesn't depress him?"

"I guess when you're pushing the century mark, you take your friends and loved ones as you find them. He'll be back before you get here. Knowing he has a visitor coming will set the stage nicely."

He put himself together, resisted an impulse to call Harriet again, and left. The drive from Century City to Woodland Hills was brief in miles, but he caught every red light several times in lockstep traffic. Motorists blew their horns, observing the fiftieth anniversary of the beginning of rush hour.

The Motion Picture Country Home is airy and spacious and beautifully maintained with funds from the actors and writers guilds and the Academy of Motion Picture Arts and Sciences. Kym was nowhere in sight, but a chubby young man in the office smiled up at him from behind a desk with a single sheet of paper on its glass top. A trivet read ASSISTANT ACTIVITIES DIRECTOR. Valentino figured the position turned over too often to bother personalizing the sign.

"Warren's expecting you," the young man said. "They only wrote down your last name. Is your first Eric, by any chance?"

"No."

"I'm sorry. His condition comes and goes. When he's not entirely, er, lucid, he keeps asking for someone named Eric. I thought it might be a family member. He seldom has visitors, so I assumed —" He shrugged. "Are you a relative?"

He gave the young man a card and the story he'd had ready. "I'm a film archivist. I understand Mr. Pegler worked in the developing lab at MGM in the twenties. I wanted to ask him some questions about early Hollywood." He was pretty sure "about a murder" would not result in an interview.

"It says on your card you're a detective."

"Show business pizzazz. *Historian* doesn't pop in this town." He made a mental note to have more pragmatic cards printed for certain venues.

"Maybe you're being too modest. You've

told me more about his professional background than he's ever told any of us, except when he's regressing, and that's usually a jumble. His file's lean on detail, but from the dates and some things he's said, it appears he was in the industry long before it was an industry. Room eighteen."

In a sunny hallway he passed a fleet of walkers and wheelchairs and the more ambulatory elderly guiding themselves along a wall rail. Some he'd met before greeted him, others he'd met before stared through him without recognition. He identified still others whose celebrity had faded ahead of them. There was more star power under that roof than anywhere else in Tinseltown, but there were no fans or paparazzi on the grounds.

Well, there was *one* fan; but for once he wasn't there to ask about gossip on the set.

A loud domestic argument seemed to be going on behind the door to eighteen. Pausing with knuckles raised inches from the panel, he heard a hysterical contralto and an infuriated baritone. Then he recognized Katharine Hepburn's Old New England accent and Humphrey Bogart's raspy lisp, and knocked loudly to make himself heard above the TV. The volume dropped and a third voice, calm as morning, told him to come in.

The old man in the wheelchair next to the bed had a full head of white hair and lively eyes in a thin, pale, pleated face. He wore a crisp dress shirt buttoned to the neck and loose tailored slacks, their legs cut off and stitched neatly at the knees, below which was nothing. A hand came up from the arm of the chair and squeezed the trigger on a long black object.

Valentino flinched; then the TV went silent, muted by the remote control in the old man's hand. On the thirty-six-inch screen, Bogie and Kate tootled without sound downriver aboard the *African Queen.*

"I don't know you."

"No, sir, we haven't met."

Warren Pegler lowered the remote. "I like to check. First my legs went, now it's my brain. One of these days they'll meet in the middle and I'll just up and disappear."

"My name is Valentino."

"No, it isn't. I'm not that far gone. He died way back when I was in physical therapy."

"Not that Valentino. I just bought the Oracle theater. I wanted to ask you some things about it as a former owner."

"You bought yourself a money hole, how's

that for starters? Cost you less just to hang a 'Rob Me' sign around your neck."

"It needs fixing up."

"I'm not talking about repairs. They're like allergies: They never go away, so you deal with them. Even fire can't break you, if you're young. It's people. Customers, distributors, building inspectors, even my own employees took everything that wasn't bolted down. My business manager skedaddled into Nazi Germany with all my investments. Stole from a cripple. I finally let the old trap go in fifty-six for less than I owed in back taxes. I thought they'd've 'dozed it by now."

"I can see why it upset you," Valentino said; although the man's bitterness showed only in his words. His tone and demeanor remained even. "Up until then, all your financial ventures were successful."

"I don't mean that. You can always recover from a bad deal. I lost my legs at eighteen and managed to get back on my feet, so to speak." He patted a stump. Then he gestured with the remote toward a picture in a silver frame on his nightstand. A big-boned unsmiling woman stared out with her hair in a French braid. "They took Gerda, too, in the end. That was the last straw. She was a strong woman; she made most of those repairs I mentioned, the ones I couldn't do with just my hands to work with. But she couldn't fix her broken heart. She just shriveled away after we lost the place."

Valentino wondered if this was what Kym Trujillo considered chipper. Yet the old man still showed no emotion.

"Why didn't you sell *Greed*? Plenty of collectors would have paid plenty for it even then." He watched closely for Pegler's reaction.

He was disappointed. The pale, pleated face was blank. "Sell greed? Times have sure changed if you can do that. Folks are generally born with it."

"I'll get to the point, Mr. Pegler." He drew up a chair that plainly had never been sat on. "A man's skeleton was found in the basement of the Oracle, along with some reels of old film. Do you know anything about it?"

"The basement? I kept all the pictures I rented in the projection room."

"Some reels showed up there as well, behind the plaster partition."

"I had Gerda put up that plaster to save on the heating bill. We didn't leave anything behind it but some empty cans."

"You overlooked some. The rest surfaced, along with the skeleton, when a wall collapsed in the basement. It was where Max Fink hid his private liquor stock during Prohibition."

"Fooling around with an old man's mind is a low thing to do, son. Especially when half of it's gone. The basement was just a basement. If there was any liquor in it I'd have drunk it up when the jackals came."

"But there wasn't any —"

The remote pointed at him again; and if it were a gun he'd be ducking. "You're asking me to take a lot at face value. *If* you're who you say you are, *if* you own the Oracle, *if* there's a skeleton and a film in a hidey-hole in the basement, that wall was there when I bought the place. You'll have to ask Max Fink. You'll find him in Forest Lawn under six feet of California."

"The brickwork in the entrance was relatively new. Anyway nowhere near as old as the building. And the skeleton —"

"A lot of people have been in and out of there since me. Maybe there were two rooms in that basement and maybe there weren't; I can't trust my memory any more than you can, but I'm not so senile I'd forget a little thing like a skeleton. Talk to the real estate people, or the movie junkies that rented the place from them, or the hippies that moved in after they left. What are you, a cop?"

Here was anger, cold as sharpened steel. Valentino sat back.

"No. I work for the UCLA Film Preservation Department. The Oracle is a personal extravagance. Naturally I'm curious about the things that came with it, but I'm more interested in you professionally. I understand you were a film technician at Metro-Goldwyn-Mayer."

Pegler rested the remote on the arm of his chair. The muscles in his face relaxed. His visitor suspected this sudden shift was a symptom of his disease. "Don't make it sound so grand," the old man said. "I was a developer, and someone's assistant at that. Young squirt that I was, I planned to run the studio one day, take Thalberg's place. Do you know Mr. Thalberg?"

The change in tenses disturbed him a little. Maybe this was one of those regressions the chubby young man in the office had mentioned. "I know of him."

"Well, ambition's one thing, luck's something else. I had too much of one and not enough of the other. Some damn fool who had no business being in the lab went out and left a cigarette burning next to fresh film stock. When the flames hit the chemicals on the shelves, the darkroom went up and me with it. They had to cut me in half to save what didn't burn." He touched the stump again, rubbed it absently.

"I'm sorry," Valentino said.

The old man looked down and saw what he was doing. For an instant he seemed to be wondering what had happened to the rest of the leg. Then he returned to the moment.

"Not necessary. I was going to direct, then produce, then buy the studio. Instead I bought a theater. Folks needed a place to go to forget when times got hard. It was a good living right up till I got robbed. Poor Gerda."

"Who's Eric?"

"Eric?"

"Someone told me you ask for him sometimes."

The confusion passed. On an old face it resembled fear. "These kids around me cackle like hens. I get my years mixed up from time to time. Eric was my first dog. Smartest Great Dane you ever saw. Hell, he's dead ninety years. Coal wagon ran over him."

"I thought it might have been Erich von Stroheim. You both worked at Metro about the same time."

"That fraud. I'd hear him snarling at my

boss outside the darkroom, coming on like the Kaiser. You couldn't print a frame fast enough to bring a smile to that fish face. Said he once belonged to Franz Josef's Imperial Guard. I bet he shoveled out the stable."

"He was a great director, though."

"DeMille was greater. He knew how to work inside a budget, and he didn't put on airs. *Von* Stroheim, my aunt's fanny. *Von* old hack."

Valentino couldn't resist. "Any DeMille stories?"

"You know that old chestnut that ends, 'Ready when you are, C. B.'?"

"Everyone must know that one by now."

"Never happened."

"Never?"

"No one on the lot ever called him C. B. Especially not a lowly second-unit cameraman. It was always Mr. DeMille. *That's* what makes a great director."

Valentino thanked him and rose. He stopped at the door. "Did you ever know a young man named Albert Spinoza? He was a projectionist."

Pegler was quiet for a moment. Then the old chin wobbled, a pathetic sight. "I'm sorry, mister, I wasn't listening. Did you say you were from Mr. Thalberg?"

He let himself out. Bogart and Hepburn resumed squabbling the moment he drew the door shut.

At the end of the hall he met Kym Trujillo carrying an armload of file folders. She was a pretty, sharp-featured brunette of thirty who had turned down a modeling job for *Sports Illustrated* to study for her MBA. *L.A. Magazine* had included her in a recent spread on Latinas who made a difference.

"How was your visit?" she asked.

"I couldn't tell when he was forgetting and when he was pretending."

"That's how you know it's one of his good days."

CHAPTER 16

Waiting in front of The Oracle for his appointment to arrive, Valentino felt his heart sink when a white stretch Mercedes limo squashed to a stop at the curb and a chauffeur got out to open the door for a small man in a three-thousand-dollar suit. The license plate read FLIX.

"Mr. Kalishnikov?" He shook a hand in a white doeskin glove. The little man wore a white fedora and a white cashmere coat over his shoulders like a cape. The temperature was eighty-six degrees in the shade, but the newcomer wasn't perspiring. Valentino was sure he couldn't afford to hire a man who didn't sweat.

"Mr. Valentino. Ha! A dead movie star and an obsolete assault weapon. Kismet! Pick me up in an hour, Rupert."

The chauffeur got in and drove away. Leo Kalishnikov surveyed the busload of chanting Berkeley students circling the sidewalk.

211

He had eyes the color of chocolate syrup and a tiny black moustache like a lowercase *w* in the middle of his round face. He was younger than expected, or else a man addicted to nips and tucks. "Who is this rabble?"

"Protesters. I can't get them to believe that skeleton didn't come over on the land bridge from Siberia twenty thousand years ago."

The little man charged up to a hulking student with hair to his shoulders and put a gloved finger to a chest in a cutoff T-shirt reading MY HEROES HAVE ALWAYS KILLED COWBOYS. "Young man, what are you protesting?"

The student wet his lips. "Four hundred years of white aggression against my people."

"I see. And you, young lady?" He turned the finger on a heavyset female with short hair and a tribal tattoo on one cheek.

"Same thing."

"I see. How about you?"

One by one, the Russian asked the same question of fourteen young people who had stopped chanting and put down their signs to provide the same answer. Kalishnikov then returned his attention to the hulk in the shoulder-length hair.

"How many parts Indian —"

"Native American." The protester bunched his chin.

"I am native Russian myself. How many parts Native American are you?"

"One-sixteenth Cherokee."

"Yes, that is the popular one. Pardon my atrocious comprehension of English and arithmetic, but do I understand that one-sixteenth of you has come here today to demonstrate against the actions of the remaining fifteen sixteenths?"

The young man opened his mouth, closed it, colored, opened it again. "Bolshevik!"

"That is very close to the word that oc-curred to me. Carry on." He led the way into the theater as if he were the host and Valentino the visitor. As the boarded-over glass door drifted shut against renewed chants from outside, Valentino said, "May I ask what the point of that was? You can't change their minds with fractions."

"Sorry I made you uncomfortable." The Russian's accent lightened, along with his diction. "Where I was born, a protest wasn't a protest if it didn't involve standing in front of a tank. Anyone can see the only Indians that bit the dust here did it up on the screen." He snatched off a glove and laid a smooth palm against the mahogany side of the ticket booth, leaving a print like a child's in the dust. "This belongs outside, under the marquee. They probably moved it to keep people from chucking rocks through the glass. See how it foreshortens the perspective in the lobby."

"Bad feng shui?"

"Actually, it cuts ten feet off what should be a journey of wonder starting at the sidewalk. The whole point of these structures was to rescue you from reality long before the lights came down and the feature rolled. Did you notice the inconsistency in the stained-glass windows?"

"Some panes are broken."

"Those can be replaced. I know a glazier in the Valley who specializes in restoring stained glass in churches and cathedrals. His shop looks like he moved it intact from eleventh-century Venice. He's expensive, but he's worth it. I was talking about the subjects: angel, angel, pastoral, knight." He turned in a circle, stabbing a finger at each of the discolored windows. "A Teutonic knight, no less; note the Maltese Cross on his breastplate. That was Fink's architect's way of preparing the patrons for the variety of the fare that awaited them. Take a good look at the fellow's face. Does he seem familiar?"

Valentino studied the stern features under the slotted visor. "He looks like Francis X. Bushman."

"Good eye. The original glazier must have gone to see *Ben-Hur* while he was working on the project. The Archangel Gabriel bears a family resemblance to the Barrymores, and unless I miss my guess that milkmaid is Mary Pickford."

"I never noticed. It's kind of tacky when you think about it."

"Tacky, yes, but with gravitas. Gothic sculptors were known to carve gargoyles into caricatures of their wealthy sponsors."

"I'm surprised Fink isn't represented. The historical commission dedicated that plaque to him much later."

"Take a closer look at winged Pegasus."

He compared the sculpture's equine features to the face on the plaque. "Holy Mother of —"

"Max. She's here, too, in plaster relief above the mezzanine entrance. I see they covered her when they suspended the ceiling over the landing. Let's hope the squirrels haven't gotten to her."

"How do you know so much about this theater? Have you been here before?"

"I never was able to work it into my schedule. I've seen so many across the country. But after we talked yesterday, I went to the Civic Center and had a long look at the building plans. They're on file there, along with the Beaudry Reservoir and Dodger Stadium."

"I was down there just the other day. I didn't think to look." Valentino paused. "You don't look like the kind of person who spends time going through dusty records."

"You should see my dry-cleaning bill. I started out in sweaters and jeans, just like any other contractor. My phone never rang. Then someone told me doing business in Hollywood is like attending one long masquerade party. So I became Vittorio De Sica out of Frank Lloyd Wright." As he spoke, Kalishnikov took off his coat, hat, and jacket, and handed them to Valentino. By the time he put his studs in a pocket and turned back his cuffs he appeared older and less pudgy; a man getting ready to go to work. "Let's assess the damage."

The archivist spent the next forty-five minutes following him around, carrying his outer clothes like a valet, while Kalishnikov pulled frayed wires spaghetti-fashion out of holes in the walls and flushed toilets and ran faucets in the restrooms and listened to the banging in the pipes as if he were a musical conductor isolating an untuned string in the violin section. It smacked faintly of affectation, but the designer muttered to himself in what sounded like peasant Russian and made close notes with a gold pencil on the inside of his starched cuffs. They covered the building from the attic, water-stained and streaked with pigeon droppings and bat guano, to the basement, where yellow police tape still festooned the room that was no longer a secret from anyone. No officers were present. Apparently the place had been squeezed dry of important clues and no one cared who tracked what onto those that remained.

The auditorium came last, as if the designer had been saving it for dessert. Valentino entered behind him hesitantly, but this time no spirits were in attendance. The tatters of the screen were blank. Kalishnikov tested the floorboards in the aisles with his weight, plucked pieces of horsehair-laced plaster from inside the proscenium arch, pounded a quart of dust out of a brittle velvet seat, and dusted off his palms. Back in the lobby he slapped the corner of a silk handkerchief at smears on his trousers and used it to wipe off his alligator shoes, patting Pegasus on the side of the neck as he did so, as if to apologize for propping his foot up on the pedestal.

"I'll do a computer search for its mate," he said, "on the long shot an employee or someone took it home to jazz up his rec room. It's custom work; there's not another like it in any theater I've been to. We'll probably have to build one from scratch. Fortunately, I know someone: Not a Michelangelo, but he could copy him so you'd never know the difference."

"In the Valley?"

"Paris."

"Paris, *France?*"

"Ornamentation's going to be the biggest part of the budget on this job. Hazmat comes next. That's asbestos dangling from the ceiling in the ladies' lounge."

"Not rock wool."

"You wish. Everything else is boilerplate: roof repair, carpentry, plumbing, and electrical. Wiring's the first order of business, to power the equipment. That means strategic drilling and snaking out the precode stuff to replace it. We want to preserve as much of the plasterwork as possible. You can't find people who can do that quality of work anymore, and even if you could, you couldn't afford them."

"I'm pretty sure I can't afford most of it."

"You might qualify for a federal loan under historic preservation."

"Can you give me a rough estimate of the cost?"

Kalishnikov took back his jacket, coat, and hat, put them on, the hat on the back of his head, produced a leather notepad with gold corners from his inside breast pocket, and scribbled on it with his gold pencil. He tore off the sheet and handed it to Valentino.

He shuddered, but his heart kept beating. "Actually, I thought it would be a lot worse."

"That's my fee. Hold on." The Russian closed his eyes, made some calculations in the air with his pencil, wrote again, and tore off the sheet.

Valentino read. He felt faint. "I don't suppose this includes your fee."

"No."

"I was afraid of that."

"*Architectural Digest* wants to do a feature on my home theaters. If you'll let them include a spread on the Oracle before and after renovation, I'll make you a present of my fee."

"I can't accept that. It's too generous."

"If you'll put that in writing, I'll throw in my expenses." Kalishnikov smiled, showing off a beautiful bond job. "I'm kidding. My last client called me a pirate, and that was for a little fifteen-seater in his basement, with a foyer and a snack bar."

"I get paid for my work. You should, too."

"I share a tax bracket with the State of North Carolina. If I make any more money this quarter, I'll have to sell the house in Malibu and set up a cot here in the lobby. I need to do the Oracle. All my work so far has been repro, on a domestic scale. I've never done a full-size theater with a legitimate history. And that murder-mystery scenario is primo advertising for my business partners."

Valentino showed his own modest dentalwork. "Are you familiar with Henry Anklemire in UCLA Information Services?"

"No."

"I think you'd get along." He folded the two pieces of paper and put them in his wallet, which was looking slim. "It's still far beyond my means, Mr. Kalishnikov. May I think about it and get back to you?"

"Certainly." The extra *y* was audible between the *t* and the *a;* the Russian had squared his hat and put on his gloves, getting into character for the protesting students, who hoisted their signs and resumed chanting slogans when the pair emerged onto the sidewalk. The limousine was waiting, Rupert the chauffeur holding the door. Valentino shook hands and watched the preposterous car bear away its preposterous passenger.

His own car released an unfamiliar odor from inside when he opened the door. The ashtray was pulled out and a cigarette lay propped across it clamped in an old-fashioned onyx holder, lisping smoke. Instinctively he glanced at the seat on the passenger's side, then at the backseat, checking for intruders. They were empty. When he looked back, the cigarette and holder were gone and the ashtray was closed.

He leaned across the driver's seat and tipped open the tray. It was clean; he didn't smoke and he'd emptied it of Broadhead's pipe ashes a day or two before. There was no cigarette or holder on the floor. It had been an optical illusion, a trick of light and shadow. Yet a faint aroma of tobacco lingered. It smelled like just the kind of exotic blend that Erich von Stroheim would have smoked in his famous holder.

"I'm doing the best I can, maestro."

Valentino slid behind the wheel, grateful for the warmth of the upholstery against his chilled spine. He opened his window to let in the combined stenches of smog and fresh-poured asphalt that bespoke West Hollywood in the twenty-first century. It wasn't enough. He needed to hear a human voice, belonging to someone of flesh and blood. In the absence of the person who'd refused all day to answer her phone, he took out his cell and dialed the office.

Ruth answered. Harriet Johansen had called, and this time the only remaining secretary on the West Coast got the name right.

CHAPTER 17

"Are you all right?" Harriet asked. "You look a little green around the gills."

They were seated in the break room down the hall from the forensics lab and the autopsy room, at a laminated table littered with copies of *Guns & Ammo, Popular Science,* and *Cinema Fantastique.* He had coffee in a Styrofoam cup. She was dipping a tea bag in a mug with her name on it.

"I'm fine. I never held a man's brains in my hands before."

"Sure? I've seen sergeants faint dead away at the first incision, twenty-year men."

"I'm fine."

"Would you like something to eat?"

"No freaking way."

She laughed.

He sipped. The stuff in the cup took skin off his tongue, but it sponged the postmortem smell from his nostrils.

A young criminalist with a puppy moustache took a bottle of water out of the refrigerator and went out, leaving them alone. Valentino reached across the table and squeezed Harriet's hand. "Thanks for forgiving me. I was too tired to remember that practical jokes always backfire on me. I don't have the talent for them."

"Peer pressure. From a twelve-year-old coed." Her eyes were still a little steely above the rim of her cup. But she didn't withdraw her hand.

"She's not much older than that, but she has a first-class brain. She's been a real help with — the program." He'd almost said *the investigation.* Even in those official surroundings, after a Cook's tour of the billion or so dollars' worth of facilities dedicated to the solution of crime in Los Angeles, it was easy to forget he was talking to an employee of the police department.

"Stop explaining before you land yourself back in the doghouse. I'm sorry I acted out. Apart from my not having the right to assume a damn thing about where this is going, playing the jealous hag is playing against type for me. I realized that even before I played back the message you left on my phone."

"That awkward thing? It was all I could do not to call back and start over."

"If you'd been glib I'd never have returned the call."

"Took you all day."

"I didn't say you didn't deserve to suffer a while."

He smiled. "So I had you at hello?"

"Make you a deal. Try not to quote movies at me and I'll try not to use words like 'postrigor putrefaction.'"

"Deal."

She slid her hand free then and wrapped it around her cup. "So what did you think of our little shop of horrors?"

"It's fascinating. But then I knew it would be. Our work isn't so different after all. We're both interested in piecing things together and preserving them. We even use some of the same equipment."

"You mean like cold-storage facilities?"

"A stand-up comic could do an hour on that with the right audience. I mean like copy cameras and electron microscopes, even scalpels. In the old days, the editors at the studios used their teeth to part the film. Having front teeth was the only prerequisite for the position. Our splicers go through several dozen disposable scalpels a day just to avoid scraping a thousandth of an inch off a single frame." He read her smile and sat back, raising his hands. "I'm hopeless, aren't I? I can't stop talking about my work even when I'm on your territory."

"We have that in common. I'm not invited to dinner parties anymore. All my former friends are afraid I'll dissect the roast to determine cause of death."

"Maybe we can wean each other off shop talk."

"Relationships have been built on less. Hello, Sergeant. What brings you downtown?"

Karen Clifford had come in, headed for the coffee machine. She changed course to stop at their table. From his seated position, Valentino looked up three feet to meet her startlingly verdant gaze. Her pile of red hair threw off halos from the fluorescents on the ceiling. "I came down to watch one of your colleagues spin sperm in a dish," she said. "That's how we investigate rape-murder now. I'm just a glorified trash collector." She offered her hand to Valentino, who rose to grasp it. "Got those reels wrapped up and ready to go? We're picking them up in the morning."

"I guess that means you didn't get anything off the cans," he said.

"We didn't expect to. We don't expect to get anything off the film, either, but we live to get lucky."

Harriet said, "I wondered about those film cans. I didn't treat them, but I saw them when they came in. *Greed;* isn't that the picture you wanted to show me last night?" She looked at him.

The sergeant lifted her chin. He was looking up at it as it was. "I didn't get an invitation to that."

"You didn't ask for it," Valentino said. "You just wanted to confiscate it."

"I still do." She looked at Harriet. "Your gentleman friend removed some evidence from the crime scene before he called us."

"I gathered that," Harriet said. "I might've been told. I've only been working the case since day one."

Valentino sensed she was angrier at Clifford for the omission than she was at him. "That was a favor to me. The film's a major find. The less it gets talked about now, the better the reception when we announce it. I was going to tell you all about it last night."

"Now that that's settled, will you surrender the evidence voluntarily, or will the officers need to bring along a warrant?"

"That won't be necessary, Sergeant. Thanks for the three days. I'm sure you took some heat over that."

She looked surprised. Then she nodded. "We'll take good care of it. We've got a cold room for perishables."

"That's only good for the short term. If it's going to run into months and years, the only really secure place to store it is in a salt mine six hundred feet deep, where there's no humidity and the temperature never rises above thirty-five degrees Fahrenheit."

"Well, we're fresh out of those. Any other tips?"

"My secretary will give your officers a copy of our department manual. The first thing to remember is not to lose the molecular sieves from the cans."

"What's a molecular sieve?"

Harriet spoke up. "It's a fancy name for those little packets they put in coat pockets to keep them from smelling musty in the stores. They allow vapors to be scavenged and contained. I'm a good listener," she explained to Valentino.

Impressed, he began to compliment her. Clifford interrupted.

"Vapors? This stuff's toxic?"

"Not yet," he said. "Not until the second stage."

"Then it's also explosive," Harriet said.

"You're pulling my leg."

They both shook their heads.

"Should I send the bomb squad to pick it up?"

Harriet spoke before Valentino could open his mouth. "Better safe than sorry."

Sergeant Clifford wandered out, forgetting the coffee machine.

Valentino sat. "You're not as good a listener as you think. That film is still a long way from volatile."

"She doesn't know that. Maybe if she thinks it is she'll tell her people to take better care of it."

"I knew you were smart. I never dreamed you were devious."

"I may be the kettle, but you're the pot. Did it ever occur to you my department will be in charge of the film, and that a word or two in my ear might improve its chances of survival? It's time you put down the cloak and dagger and come clean."

"You're mixing metaphors."

"BS."

"Excuse me?"

"I'm a bachelor of science, not arts. I can mix metaphors the same way I mix chemicals and compounds." She took the tea bag out of her cup, sucked it, and laid it on the table. He'd never seen anyone do that before; they were a matched set of caffeine addicts. "I try to keep an open mind," she went on. "That's why I let you talk your way out of that stupid misunderstanding yesterday. That doesn't mean I'll let you keep half your life hidden from me. Even the moon shows its dark side once a night."

"Douglas the negative cutter must've really done a number on you," he said.

"Several. One of them was changing the subject every time the conversation became uncomfortable."

He lifted his cup. It was cold. "Is it all right if I warm this up first?"

"Dump it out and bring me more hot water while you're up." She pushed her cup toward him and fished another tea packet out of a pocket in her smock.

He talked all through both beverages. He told her about the scheme to smuggle out *Greed* before calling the police and the decision to investigate the mystery of the skeleton. He left out the tentative identification of Albert Spinoza as the victim and his interview with Warren Pegler, but only because Fanta had brought those about through skills he couldn't claim and he didn't want to jeopardize her future as an attorney; he didn't know Harriet well enough yet to trust her with someone else's fate. About himself he was candid.

He even told her about the ghost.

He almost didn't. It was okay if his friends thought he was a screwball; the local landscape was filled with those. He risked losing Harriet's interest on the grounds of sheer humdrummery.

"The first time was in my apartment, the night of the day I bought the Oracle and found the film and the skeleton. I was in bed, so I put it down as a dream. Von Stroheim was in full costume, complete with monocle and riding breeches. He asked — commanded me to save *'mein Kindling,'* meaning his beloved child: *Greed.*"

"He spoke in German? Do you know the language?"

"I studied it in high school. I've forgotten most of what I learned. Fortunately, he only used a phrase or two. The rest was in English."

She nodded, encouraging him to continue.

"I saw him the second time in the theater just after you left. That time I knew I was awake. He was all in pieces on the torn fabric of the movie screen, but I could see he was dressed like Gloria Swanson's butler in *Sunset Boulevard.*"

"I thought it was Norma Desmond."

"That was the character. Swanson played her. Can I tell this? It's difficult enough."

"Sorry. I'll try not to talk during the movie."

"It was pretty much the same conversation," he said; leaving out the personal part where von Stroheim told him to avoid feminine distraction. "He wasn't satisfied with the progress I was making, which was in character for him. He could delay an expensive production to correct some minor detail on the set, but if an actor was on his mark three minutes late he flew into a rage. Only this time I knew it wasn't a dream, because I was awake and on my feet." He searched her face for traces of mockery. He found none. "The third time was today, in my car. I didn't really see him that time, just the cigarette he left behind in one of those hokey holders. I guess he got tired of waiting."

"Did you keep the cigarette and holder?"

"No. They disappeared before I could reach for them."

"Too bad. We could've identified the tobacco, tested for latents, analyzed the saliva on the holder for DNA, matched it to a relative or a lock of hair in someone's locket, and determined whether it was von Stroheim who smoked it."

"I was afraid you'd make a joke."

"That's what ghosts are, a joke. Did you

expect me to invite you to a séance? I haven't lived here long enough to catch that disease. I still have my South Dakota immunity."

"Fanta and Dr. Broadhead weren't so quick to dismiss the supernatural angle."

"Neither one of them is a scientist. I believe in things I can put under a microscope or on litmus or spin in a dish."

"What about God?"

"That's faith. I leave it in my locker when I put on the smock."

"Maybe this is one of those times you should take it off."

"Not unless you think God wears a monocle and speaks with a thick German accent."

"Austrian, actually. The only time he played a German was in *Five Graves to Cairo,* when he was General Rommel." He saw her expression. "Sorry. At least I didn't quote from the film."

"Do you think you saw a ghost?"

He considered. Neither Broadhead nor Fanta had asked that question.

"No," he said. "Everything I've ever read about real-life sightings is vague. This was as vivid as if I were watching a movie."

"You're overwrought. My gosh, from what you said, Webster's should put your picture in the dictionary next to the definition. Since movies are your main point of reference, you put all your anxieties into a cinematic context. In your position, I'd be seeing dancing test tubes everywhere I went."

"Even when I'm awake?"

"I can't speak for what shape you were in today, but you looked kind of wasted that day at the theater. I used to doze off sitting at my desk at USC after pulling an all-nighter with the books. My head never touched the desk."

"Dr. Broadhead suggested sleepwalking."

"It's more common than you think. Why do you think von Stroheim used only as much German as you still retained from high school? That was as much as your subconscious mind gave him access to."

He blinked. "Wow. I never thought of that."

"You're not haunted." She reached across the table and took both his hands in hers. "And you're not crazy."

Crazy about you, he thought; but it was too early for that. Instead he squeezed her hands. "If I ever feel I'm slipping, I'll run straight to you. Anyone who'd run a DNA test on a spook could talk me sane."

"Mr. Valentino, that's just about the sweet-

est thing anyone ever told a forensic pathologist." She glanced around the empty
room, then leaned forward and pressed her
lips to his.

CHAPTER 18

Valentino had timed himself to arrive late the next morning; but the LAPD, evidently determined to spare him nothing, was behind schedule as well. After his daily exchange of unpleasantries with the grumpy parking attendant, he emerged on foot from the garage in time to see a bearing party of officers in helmets and flak jackets lugging carton after carton from the preservation building to an armor-plated SUV parked in front. Sergeant Clifford seemed to have accepted Harriet's assessment of the cargo at face value.

Ruth ambushed him from behind her desk in the old power plant. "You're late. The joint's been raided."

He'd guessed they'd been there first, from the amount of mud that had been tracked onto the floor downstairs. A misty rain had been falling all morning. "It was expected. Didn't Dr. Broadhead warn you?"

"They tramped in while he was talking. I haven't seen so many cops in one place since they arrested John Landis."

That would be for the accident that killed Vic Morrow and two child extras on the set of *Twilight Zone — The Movie.* He'd had no idea her studio experience had lasted so late. "He was acquitted," he said. "We should have such luck. Where's Dr. Broadhead?"

"He went with them."

"Don't tell me they arrested *him.*" He had a sudden horrible picture of his friend refusing to cooperate, reliving the martyrdom of his younger years.

"He took them over to the lab. Here he is now."

The professor strolled in in hat, trench coat, and rubbers, puffing his pipe. Ruth, who had appointed herself monitor of the university's smoke-free policy, scooped a heavy ashtray out of a drawer and thrust it at him. Meekly he rapped the smoldering dottle out into the tray and watched her stab at the glowing ash with the eraser end of a pencil.

Valentino said, "I was afraid I was going to have to go downtown and bail you out."

"It was extraordinary," Broadhead said. "They came with dozens of cartons, enough to clean out the entire library. I suspect they were misled to believe they were here to confiscate *Foolish Wives*. You know, the sour Kraut shot three *hundred* reels before Thalberg shut him down that time. No one seems to care about recovering those. Discrimination seems to be gaining ground even among fanatics."

"What happened?"

"Well, he began by rebuilding Monte Carlo from the ground up and then filming a reel of establishing footage before he got three yards inside the door. Things escalated from —"

"I mean with the police!"

"Oh. Most civilized. There's not a Barton MacLane or a Bill Demarest to be found among this polite college-educated breed. I supervised the loading, and the fellow in charge, a sergeant named Masserian, kept inventory and gave me a copy with a signed receipt. The vandals who moved Elaine and me into our house could have taken lessons from the way this crew handled the merchandise. There wasn't a dramatic moment, in case you were afraid you'd missed anything." He fixed Valentino with his bland gaze.

"I missed it on purpose. I hate attending funerals."

"I hope you'll make an exception in the case of mine. I've made some alterations in the text."

"I wish I had your sense of humor. I can't find a single thing to smile about this morning."

Ruth said, "I sure can't. I'm not getting much work done in this gabfest."

"Step into my office," Broadhead told Valentino.

"Let's step into mine. Today of all days I need my personal clutter about me."

"What do you suppose she finds to work on? I write all my letters, and you're never around long enough to hitch her to the plow." Broadhead made himself comfortable in his usual seat and began packing his pipe.

Valentino said, "Would you mind not doing that? Rebellion gets old fast."

Broadhead raised his bushy brows, then shrugged and laid the pipe in the Schwab's saucer where his friend kept paper clips. "You behave as if I'm the only revolutionary in situ," he said. "How's progress with the Oracle Murder Case?" He made it sound like a lost Philo Vance title.

"We may have identified the victim. And we found Warren Pegler. That is to say Fanta found him. I interviewed him yesterday at the Country Home."

"He's alive? Dear me. Does this mean I have to look forward to shaving this face for another few decades?"

Valentino filled him in on Albert Spinoza and what he'd gotten from Pegler. The old man's information sounded even more meager in summary.

"Do you suspect him?" Broadhead asked.

"I don't know. Diminished capacity can be a real advantage during interrogation."

"Did you tell any of this to the Big Red Dog?"

"I ran into Clifford last night at headquarters. I never thought about it, to be honest. We were making arrangements for her to seize *Greed.* That was very civilized, too. You'd have been proud of my behavior."

"I am. There's no sense making a scene when you're surrounded by people with guns and handcuffs. What were you doing at headquarters?"

"I was there for that tour Harriet promised."

"Elucidate." He never sounded more the professor taking a pupil through his lessons.

"It was illuminating. Did you know you can track a suspect's movements over the past year by analyzing the wax in his ear?"

"Stop being so romantic. Did you get to

first base?"

Valentino colored. For the first time in their long acquaintance, Broadhead's brows made contact with his shaggy hairline. He laughed sincerely, loud and booming. Out in the hall, Ruth pounded her foot for silence.

"Right brain meets left," he said, wiping tears from his eyes. "Your children will spend all day in the video store and all night scraping the discs to see what makes them work."

"That's out of line, even for you. I apologized for asking about you and Fanta."

Subdued, Broadhead tugged at the hem of his sweater-vest. "How did your meeting go with Kalishnikov? I hear he's eccentric. When a second-unit AD at Fox complained about his bill, he had the equipment and furnishings ripped out and turned the theater back into a storeroom, with the original junk. He went to the landfill to retrieve it personally."

"He probably started that rumor himself. He's a pro in parvenu clothing." Valentino took one of the slips out of his wallet and passed it across the desk.

"What's this, the population of Santa Monica?"

"That's his fee. He offered to waive it if I

let him use the Oracle in his promotion."

"He *is* eccentric. Of course you accepted." He placed the estimate atop the pile of papers on the desk.

"Even if I did, the actual work would put me into debt beyond the grave."

"If you made that calculation, you must be considering going ahead."

Valentino shook his head. "I'm thinking of selling the place to someone who can afford to restore it."

"Anyone with that kind of money would be smart enough to level it and put up an office building on the site. You'd never forgive yourself."

"The other day you tried to talk me into forgetting the whole thing."

Broadhead picked up his pipe and straightened out a paper clip to probe inside the stem. "As your only friend, I have the responsibility to perform as your Greek chorus. If I thought you'd take the advice, I wouldn't have offered it. When God goes out of His way to hand you an epiphany, turning it down would only tick Him off."

"That's the second time God's come up in conversation in the last twelve hours. I thought this was a secular town."

"Balderdash. Every time someone with a bright line of patter throws a butt into the gutter on Cahuenga, a dozen people swarm around it to erect a shrine. My mailman can't deliver my utility bill because the box is stuffed with circulars predicting the end of the world; even the Apocalypse has its positive side. Bite the bullet, Val. If you start moping around wringing your hands because some practical type built yet another Comerica Bank on hallowed Hollywood ground, I'll have to strike up a conversation with Ruth just to break the monotony."

Valentino smiled despite himself. "Well, we can't have that."

"I knew you'd come to your senses if I put it in an altruistic context. A personal relationship with Ruth could drive me back to the classroom. Have you given any more thought to selling *Greed* to the university?"

"Pegler said you shouldn't have to sell greed since it isn't in short supply. Apparently I've got my share. Do you really think I can get fifty thousand?"

"You can get double, but don't tell the department head I said that. He already thinks we're all going to be selling flowers on the entrances to the San Diego Freeway if the Democrats don't get back in next time around."

"I couldn't ask for a hundred. I feel like a traitor considering any price at all."

"Next week, some stinking rich alumnus fresh out of white-collar prison will present the president with a giant novelty check, and every third-string player on the football team will have his own personal jacuzzi. UCLA will survive. So will the Oracle; but only if you stop thinking of *Greed* as if it were the Wailing Wall and treat it as the commodity it was intended to be."

Valentino watched him puttering with his pipe, the only fetish in his acerbic, ascetic life. "You're a good friend, Kyle."

"Your *only* friend. You can't count Harriet Johansen yet. She's still your Dulcinea at this early stage."

"You forgot Kym Trujillo at the Country Home."

"Have you ever had dinner at her house? Or had her to dinner at yours?"

"Lunch, a couple of times."

"Lunch is a bribe, to patch up the pipeline to your best source of anecdotal information. Did you tell her about your ghost?"

"Of course not."

"I rest my case. How is old Erich, by the way? Dead and well, I trust? In good spirits?"

"I missed him last time. He left his smoking paraphernalia in my car, but only for a moment."

"Um." Broadhead sucked on the cold pipe. "I wouldn't think an apparition had any pressing engagements."

"When I said you were a good friend, I was referring to your efforts to distract me from the thought that right now a bunch of day laborers with flat feet and a taste for deep-fried pastry are putting their ham fists all over the find of two centuries."

"Snobbery doesn't become you. As a matter of fact, many of L.A.'s finest are blessed with admirably high arches. As to the value of the confiscated property, I have my doubts; although dogs are universally popular. You said Pegler still mourns the one he lost to a coal wagon ninety years ago."

"What do dogs have to do with *Greed*?"

"Nothing, in context. Gluttony's as close as they come to that human sin. But I do expect a proper demonstration of wrath when Sergeant Clifford and her people get past the first three reels and find themselves following the adventures of Rin-Tin-Tin."

Valentino sat up. "Elucidate."

"History has largely forgotten that before the brothers Warner greenlighted *The Jazz Singer,* rescuing us all from the poetry of silence, the exploits of a heroic German shepherd were all that stood between them and bankruptcy. They ran that studio on a shoestring and gallons of red ink."

"Tell me you didn't put Rin-Tin-Tin in those cans before you let them go."

"Very well. I did not."

"Kyle!"

"Assuming you wish to rephrase that as a question, I will respond that I did not do that solely. I'm no piker, and anyway I couldn't fill all forty-two cans with less than three thousand feet of film. I put in reels one, two, and three of *Greed,* which we'd just barely transferred to safety, threw in the dog, and finished out the bill with *Tarzan of the Apes,* starring the immortal Elmo Lincoln, his leopard skin, and his beer belly. Grand stuff, and we've got it all on backup. What more could you ask, short of a travelogue, a newsreel, and Porky the Pig?"

Valentino cursed loud and long. Ruth pounded.

"I considered *The Perils of Pauline,*" Broadhead said, "but it doesn't date nearly as well. I have standards."

A fist slammed the desk, starting a paperslide of scripts and playbills that continued long into the speech that followed. "This isn't a fraternity prank. We started out by withholding evidence, now we're tampering with it. Clifford's smart enough to spot the difference between Zasu Pitts and a police dog."

"Debatable. Pitts was no great beauty. But *Greed*'s safe in our hands, and posterity will judge whether it's more important to punish a murderer or save a masterpiece."

"You're wrong. A judge will judge, and you and I will be watching all our movies in the San Quentin cafeteria. And how did *Greed* manage that tricky U-turn back to masterpiece? A few minutes ago it was a commodity."

"I was speaking for posterity, not myself. Anyway, it won't even be a commodity if we let them stick it in the refrigerator with the tuna sandwiches. Your view of penal life is confined to the screen, incidentally. If you don't actually shiv someone in the shower room, they pipe basic cable into your cell. *Citizen Kane* with feminine hygiene spots is better than no *Kane* at all." Broadhead scratched the side of his nose with the paper clip, leaving an ashen mark. "But that's my burden. You'll be in your own Xanadu, fighting with building inspectors, while I'm busy rattling my cup against the bars, demanding more gruel." He cocked his head. "No, that's *Oliver Twist*. It's high time I retired to the rock pile. I can no longer distinguish between Jackie Coogan and

Jimmy Cagney."

"If you think I'm going to stand by and let you take the rap alone —"

"Spoken like George Raft. It's not your choice. I'll exonerate you in my confession. I won't have you playing Cook to my Peary and smudging my individual achievement."

"Don't you mean your martyrdom?"

"The image is inconsistent. Cook and Peary were explorers, not martyrs. Those don't come in pairs. Which was the whole point of my argument." He smiled his baggy academic smile. "Don't weep for me. The cell is bound to be more comfortable than that Eastern European dungeon, and if I can resist the temptation to crash the gate, the warden may let me have paper and pencils to finish my book. A lot of great literature has been created behind bars: *Don Quixote,* the stories of O. Henry, *The Gulag Archipelago.*"

"You left out *Mein Kampf.*"

"Hitler's style meandered too much to qualify. Anyway, that whole Holocaust thing detracts from the text. Mad dictators should hire ghosts to write their memoirs; meaning no offense to Herr von Stroheim."

"Heroes make a difference. That's how you know they're heroes. You'll just be a drain on the taxpayers while Clifford gets a court order and takes the film anyway."

"That's her privilege. We'll have it on safety by the time my trial date is set. The publicity alone should encourage our president to put the entire technical staff on the job and step up the pace."

Valentino said, "I know just how he'll feel."

"Meaning what?"

"Meaning you just doubled my determination to solve this case before they drag you away to jail."

Broadhead tapped a tooth with the mouthpiece of his pipe. "Can I play too?"

CHAPTER 19

Fanta joined them at the microbrewery downtown, where the bunkerlike atmosphere of booths and conversational buzz provided a comfortable environment for plotting strategy. They'd hoped for a spot by the picture of Basil Rathbone with deerstalker and pipe, but that was occupied by some mid-level studio executives scribbling new dialogue on a script with a pen borrowed from their waitress. The trio settled for one near the kitchen under the sardonic supervision of Warren William.

"Didn't he play Sam Spade once?" Fanta asked.

"Badly," Broadhead said.

"Perfect," said Valentino. "He won't show us up."

The men ordered beers, the young woman iced tea, and they shared a platter of ethnic samplers, referred to in the menu as the Our Gang Plate. Valentino watched the professor strip all the greenery from a pita sandwich. "Why the change of heart? You've been riding me with Junior G-Man jokes all week. Now you're joining the squad."

"That was work, this is play. I told you my job is to be the wise Fool to your King Lear."

"You said you were the Greek chorus."

"They provide the same stage business. In any case it's been no fun hovering upstage. I want to share the center spot."

Fanta said, "Do you two think we can restrict the analogies to the movies? I was just starting to recognize some of them, and now you ring in Aeschylus and Shakespeare." She colored when the men stared at her. "Okay, I went for a theater major my freshman year. I was going to be the next Barrymore."

"John or Ethel?" They said it together.

"Drew. I got a shot of good sense up the ying-yang when I auditioned for *Marat/Sade* in the school play."

"Was that Dr. Zinnerman's production?" Broadhead asked.

"Yes. Did you see it?"

"I never go to the theater: too much yelling and stomping about. But Zinnerman's the nastiest piece of work on the faculty. If he taught law instead of drama, he'd have humiliated you out of going for that degree."

"No way. He was a bear, but he did me a favor. I might have wasted a whole semester finding out I've got less talent in my whole body than Lynn Fontanne has in her dead little finger."

"Is that how he put it?"

"He used adjectives. Mr. Yardley was plenty tough in the class I took from him on contract law, but he couldn't shake me. I aced the final."

"That's impressive," Broadhead said. "Jack Yardley started out as a criminal attorney, reducing mob killers to tears during cross-examination. And he hands out A's the way Fort Knox gives free samples."

Valentino said, "Maybe we should invite him in."

"Ew," Fanta said. "I bet he hasn't trimmed the hair in his nose since his bar exam."

The professor finished weeding his pita. "A distinct advantage in court. It's almost impossible to get a jury to pay attention to your summation when they're watching your opponent marcelling his nostrils at the defense table."

"Charming." Valentino pushed away his plate of angel hair pasta.

Fanta drank iced tea. She wore a tank top and cargo pants and her black hair loose to her shoulders, a hooded cellophane raincoat flung over the back of her seat. It was an incongruous mix with the woven-leather shoulder bag beside her on the cushion. The bag was the same one she'd had with her the day she and Valentino had started their investigation. The young studio executives looked up frequently from the script they were mutilating to cast admiring glances her way. She appeared oblivious to their interest. "I like this place," she said. "It reminds me of the pub in *The Invisible Man*. I've been boning up on old videos."

Valentino said, "They built it on top of a cocktail bar. William Holden drank himself to death at a corner table."

"I thought he got drunk and fell down in his apartment."

"He was already half embalmed when he left here."

"Charming." Broadhead set down his beer untasted. "*The Invisible Man* isn't a murder mystery," he told Fanta.

"I know, but I fell in love with Claude Rains's voice when I saw *Deception*. You don't hear pipes like that anymore, and we had some great ones in drama class."

"Microphones," said Broadhead. "No reason thundering out to the back row when you're wearing a lavalier around your neck."

From there the talk turned to other great stage-trained voices, Rathbone's and Welles's and Edward Arnold's. It was Valentino who steered it back to the business at hand. "Let's review what we've got so far."

"Not much," Fanta said. "A newspaper article about a missing projectionist who fits the skeleton's description and what Warren Pegler told you." He'd filled her in on the interview while they were waiting for the booth.

"What he didn't tell me amounts to a lot more," Valentino said.

Their waitress, older and more ambitious than the woman who'd served them the other day, asked if they wanted anything else, took orders for coffee and a refill of Fanta's tea, and left, bearing away their dishes.

"Maybe this'll help." Fanta dragged the shoulder bag onto her lap and opened the clasp. Valentino half expected her to produce another coffee table book with a picture of The Oracle in its glory, but instead she drew out a thick padded mailer and tipped a pile of folio-size newspapers onto the freshly cleared table. They smelled musty and the brittle old pulp was crumbling at the folds, but the heavy black masthead, identical on all three, still screamed for attention:

The edition on top of the slanted stack was dated January of that same year.

"I tracked it down through the Smithsonian Web site," she said. "An online book finder found it for me in a shop in Las Cruces, New Mexico, of all places, and had them overnight it: the entire run, all three issues."

Broadhead picked up the top copy and unfolded it to study a grainy photo of a pair of corpses in hats and overcoats sprawled on the bullet-riddled front porch of a miniature Spanish hacienda. MEX SPEAK SERVES UP 2 STIFF ONES, read the caption.

"Offhand, I'd say they overestimated their readership when they named the rag."

"There were dozens of these little dudes floating around town those days," Fanta said. "When I found that out, I started wondering if some of their editors didn't flip the bird at the studios and their control of the press."

"Flipping the bird was the tabloids' specialty," Broadhead said, "although they usually selected safer targets, like cops and gangsters. Picking on Hollywood might explain why this one ran only three issues." He spread it open to an inside page. "Oh, look. Calvin Coolidge in a Sioux warbonnet."

Valentino felt a little buzz of anticipation, as if he were homing in on a Griffith reel. "What made you choose this one?"

"I didn't. It chose me. This isn't the only package I got. My floor at home is covered with old newspapers. Now my side looks just like my roommate's."

"How much did all that cost?" he asked her.

"Let's just say my parents are getting McDonald's gift certificates for Christmas this year."

Broadhead closed and folded *The Angel City Intelligencer.* "That's extravagant, young lady. At your age you should be blowing textbook money on keggers."

She screwed up her face and stuck out her tongue between her teeth. The professor sighed heavily.

"Good heavens, look at those old newspapers! Is one of us a scrapbooker?"

All three looked up at their waitress, who moved the stack to set down the coffees and iced tea.

"I'm thinking of taking it up," Broadhead said. "My doctor says I need to find a hobby less strenuous than Civil War reenactment. Carrying around that sword is murder on the sacroiliac."

"Just make sure you seal it all in archival plastic. The older the material, the sooner it deteriorates."

He thanked her for the advice.

When they were alone again, Valentino said, "Civil War reenactment?"

"My idiot older brother. He died at Gettysburg for Selznick and again at Shiloh for John Huston."

"How old *are* you?"

"Older than Ruth and younger than San Jacinto." He looked at Fanta. "Are you going to guide us to the truth, or must we spend all day improving our education on flappers and philosophers?"

"I'm not sure I know what that means, but here." She slid out the February issue, opened it to an inside page, folded it carefully into a square, and passed it across to Broadhead. Valentino leaned over his shoulder to read the square two-column item in the lower lefthand corner:

REEL-LIFE SCOUNDREL PROVES REAL-LIFE HERO

Erich von Stroheim, billed in theaters as

"The Man You Love to Hate" for his numerous portrayals of villains on the silver screen, reversed roles to save the life of a fellow studio employee during a fire on the MGM lot late last month.

Unnamed sources report that when a blaze broke out in the film developing laboratory, actor-director von Stroheim, who was present, disregarded his own life and safety to pull an assistant developer from the blaze.

Von Stroheim received minor burns during the rescue. Warren Pegler, 18, was taken by ambulance to Los Angeles General Hospital, where his condition is still critical. The cause of the fire is under investigation, although inspectors suspect careless smoking was involved.

The text surrounded a cropped photograph of von Stroheim that Valentino recognized from the director's early days at Universal, wearing a monocle and a well-cut tweed suit and carrying a walking stick, a Tyrolean hat at an arrogant angle on his bullet-shaped head. He had the ubiquitous cigarette and holder clamped between a thumb and forefinger.

"I can't understand why MGM suppressed the story in the bigger papers,"

Fanta said. "Nowdays it would be all over *ET* and *People.* Von Stroheim rocked."

Broadhead said, "Nowadays, studios have insurance. Careless smoking is serious negligence. If a personal injury attorney had gotten wind of it, the suit would have cost millions, and the trial would have dragged on for weeks on every front page in the country, smearing the industry at a time when it couldn't afford another witch hunt. It was lucky this got lost in the tabloid avalanche." He looked up from the page. "You've unearthed a previously undiscovered piece of cinema history. That's like finding a nugget the Forty-Niners overlooked. Think you can handle a second major?"

Smiling, she propped her chin on her palm. "Tell you after I finish making up for all the homework I blew off this week."

"She's done more than just add to Hollywood lore," Valentino said. "She's established a direct link between Warren Pegler and Erich von Stroheim. It can't be coincidence we found *Greed* in the Oracle."

"I've been wondering about that," Fanta said. "The theater, I mean. You said Pegler told you his business manager took off for Nazi Germany with all his investments?"

"That's what he said."

"I should've paid more attention during Western History. Didn't the Nazis surrender in, like, nineteen forty-four?"

"Forty-five." Broadhead drank coffee. "According to my great-grandmother."

"So what kept him going till he sold the place in fifty-six?"

"Tickets and popcorn," Broadhead said.

"It wouldn't have been enough." Valentino sat back. "The book Fanta gave me said the Oracle was one of the first movie houses in L.A. to install Cinerama and three-D projectors and stereophonic speakers, to compete with television. The retrofitting alone would have cost him thousands, just at the time he said he was struggling. Why didn't I think of that when I was asking him questions?"

Broadhead said, "You're an archivist, not a criminal investigator, no matter what your cards say. You're not used to tripping people up in their lies. Most of the old-timers you talk to have been waiting years for an audience they haven't told the same stories to a hundred times. The trick is getting them to shut up."

"Kym Trujillo told me he has his good days and his bad. I thought I was lucky to catch him on one of the good ones. It never occurred to me they'd be better than mine."

"So let's catch him on one of the bad ones," Broadhead said. "You said he's at his best in the morning?"

"That's what Kym said. Should we pay a call on him this afternoon?"

Fanta broke in. "You really suspect this guy of killing Spinoza?"

"There's no real reason to," Valentino said. "We don't have a motive. But there's no law against hoarding a classic film, and homicide's the only thing he'd have to be shifty about after all these years. There's no statute of limitations, and his room is a lot more comfortable than a prison cell."

"Not to bum you out, but Pegler was more than twice Spinoza's age in fifty-six, an old man —"

"Middle-aged, mathematically speaking," Broadhead said. "He's lived almost as long since."

"— a middle-aged man in a wheelchair, with no legs. I'm the jury. Convince me he cracked his projectionist over the head and walled him up in the basement. How'd he get down all those stairs?"

Broadhead nodded. "You're good. Forget what I said about a second major."

Gloom settled over the booth. Their waitress, sensing the mood, left their check and drifted away without a word.

Valentino perked up. "We'll ask Pegler. Or maybe you should, a proper cross-examination. It could be extra credit toward your degree."

"At the risk of talking you out of it, shouldn't we put this in Sergeant Clifford's hands?"

Broadhead and Valentino exchanged guilty glances. The professor cleared his throat. "We're avoiding the police right now." He told her about his bait-and-switch.

"You're just a naughty old man, aren't you?" she said.

"Middle-aged."

"I'll call Kym." Valentino took out his cell.

"Time enough for that later," Broadhead said. "We have a stop to make first."

"Where?"

"The wardrobe department at Universal. I know someone there. This was a less informal town in Pegler's day. You need to dress appropriately."

"Why don't I just swing by my place and put on a tie?"

"No offense, but styles have changed, and not for the better. First impressions count."

"This is my second visit."

"Well, you know what they say about Alzheimer's: You meet new people every day."

"That's incredibly insensitive. What about

you and Fanta? You're not exactly dressed for an audience with royalty."

"We don't want to overcostume the thing. Too much period detail can drag down a production. Ask von Stroheim about that next time you see him."

"What are you up to?"

Broadhead shoved the bill his way. "Just pay that. I'll take care of the rest."

"Hold still, Professor." Fanta wet a corner of a napkin in her glass and reached across to wipe the smudge of ash off the side of Broadhead's nose. "That's been making me non compos mentis for like an hour."

It had been bothering Valentino too, ever since his friend had scratched his nose with the paper clip he'd used to clean his pipe, but he hadn't the courage to say or do anything about it. He braced for a curmudgeonly outburst. Instead, Broadhead looked sheepish and got up without a word to retrieve his hat and trench coat.

■ ■ ■ ■

IV
RED CARPET

■ ■ ■ ■

CHAPTER 20

At the gate to Universal City, the guard, a youngster good-looking enough to have a resume and head shots in his locker, spoke Kyle Broadhead's name into his telephone, waited through what seemed to be a series of connections, spoke again, listened, and wrote out passes for all three of them. Then he activated a motor that whirred and clunked like the gate mechanism in a prison film. Valentino drove through the opening.

"Cool," said Fanta, when they passed a group of extras in French Foreign Legion uniforms. "You think we'll get to see the shark?"

Broadhead said, "That's in Florida."

"Don't tell me you never took the tour," said Valentino.

"I said I'm a Hollywood brat. If I lived in San Antonio I'd never have gotten to visit the Alamo."

Security was tight; the industry was convinced it was a top terrorist target. They were stopped by guards twice and asked to show their passes and driver's licenses. The parking attendant checked them out again and smacked a pink sticker with the day's date to the windshield. They found a space far down from the Hummers and Testarossas, next to a spotless Mercedes with the features and options still glued to a window.

"A writer," Broadhead said. "Poor slob."

Rain was still falling, one of those all-day mists that are as rare in Southern California as natural redheads. "There's luck."

Broadhead's companions looked to him for explanation. He offered none.

At the door to the wardrobe department they handed their credentials to a square-shouldered man in a blue suit with a corkscrew wire coming out of his ear. He asked them each for a date of birth, compared it to the license, and handed it back. He thanked them politely and muttered into his fist. A buzzer sounded. He pushed the door open and held it. The visitors passed through.

Fanta said, "I hope that's the last of it. I'm wearing granny panties."

They were in a hangarlike room that appeared to be a combination clothing warehouse and garment district sweatshop, only one with superior working conditions. Aisles of bare floor wandered between racks of costumes on casters, and hundreds, possibly thousands more suits, dresses, cloaks, leotards, and menageries of animal prints hung from tubes that circled the walls in stacks to the ceiling; as Valentino and Fanta followed Broadhead, the center row glided under its own power to the accompaniment of a humming motor, rotating its selection of textiles nearly halfway around the enormous room before it stopped and a woman on a catwalk removed a sequined evening gown on its hanger, folded it over one arm, and descended a flight of stairs to the floor. Bolts of fabric covered tables as large as full-size beds for cutters armed with shears, and tailors and seamstresses sat at columns of whirring sewing machines, feeding yards of silk, wool, and man-made materials to the bobbins. In spite of an elaborate ventilation system of ceiling fans and built-in air filters, the great room smelled of sizing, starch, and model airplane glue.

"Awesome," Fanta said.

Valentino, who had visited before, could supply no better word to describe it.

"This is the largest unit in the plant," Broadhead said, "or it was anyway before they added a computer-generated special effects department, which is about as interesting to watch at work as a microwave oven. They go through more than eight hundred thousand yards of cloth here each year. Theoretically, that would clothe the population of La Jolla."

"The population of La Jolla can afford its own clothes," Fanta pointed out.

"Barstow, then. That's the core of the reference library there. A good portion of it is chronically overdue on the shelves in the designers' offices."

Under the catwalk that circled the room one story high, sturdy steel shelves arranged in stacks perpendicular to the walls supported rank after rank of books, some as small as change purses and crusted with gilding, many as large as world atlases. Some were very old and still wore the rings that had been used to chain them to medieval reading desks. There were nearly as many volumes in the room as there were articles of clothing.

"It's an unholy mess right now," said a new voice. "We're in the middle of switching from Dewey Decimal to Library of Congress. I spent all day yesterday looking for the last century of the Roman Empire. Hello, Kyle, you look like James Thurber." A silver-haired woman in glasses with round heavy black rims abandoned a paper pattern spread out on a cutting table to come forward and grasp the professor's hand. She wore a smock from neck to heels, stained with a rainbow spectrum of dyes.

Broadhead, in his trenchcoat and bucket hat, chuckled malevolently. "I see you're still wearing Edith Head's prescription."

"Just the glasses. Don't spread it around, but they were a prop. Windowpane lenses." She tapped hers, which were as thick as shuffleboard shuttles and no windowpanes. "What's so urgent I had to postpone Sandy Bullock?"

"I love her," Fanta said.

"You never had to fit her." She slid down her glasses and surveyed the young woman head to foot. "Size four."

"Two."

"Want to bet?"

"How much?"

"You'd lose," Broadhead told Fanta. "Meet Sister Agnes, the finest wardrobe mistress in the business. She put Buster Keaton's hat on Johnny Depp in *Benny and Joon*. The rest is Hollywood history." He introduced Fanta and Valentino.

"That was at Metro." The woman didn't shake hands. "And I'm a costume technician. Wardrobe mistresses went out with

271

blackface."

"Right on, sister," said Fanta.

"Are you a nun?" asked Valentino.

"I'm Presbyterian. I took my vows at Our Lady of Perpetual Alteration."

"She got the monicker when she slapped Mickey Rourke across the knuckles with a tape measure," Broadhead said. "That's when they asked her to leave Metro."

"They asked me back after Rourke crashed and burned, but I'd just finished reorganizing this rattrap." Pointedly she checked the watch she had pinned to a lapel.

Broadhead told the others to take the tour. "I'm going to tell Sister Agnes what we want."

"Maybe then you'll tell us," Valentino said.

Fanta tugged at his sleeve. "Let's browse. This is like being locked up in a toy shop."

They walked away, leaving the professor and the ersatz nun conversing in low tones.

"What's he up to now?" Valentino asked.

"If it's no worse than a misdemeanor, he's heading in the right direction. Wicked! Check it out."

While she admired a spaghetti-strap dress with a label sewn inside reading J. ROBERTS/ERIN BROCKOVICH, he wandered toward a triptych mirror mounted on a carpeted platform, where a former member of the ensemble cast of a hit sitcom whose name he couldn't remember was being fitted for yet another incarnation of a Jane Austen classic.

The actor fussed with his breeches. "Man, these are *tight*. How do you, um . . . ?"

"Peel them down and squat, both functions." The young man kneeling at his feet took a pin from his mouth and transfixed a loose seam. "Picture Mr. Darcy doing that in Technicolor."

Valentino rapped a knuckle on a Trojan breastplate on a torso form and got the hollow thump of papier-mâché. A mannequin dressed for evening told him Al Pacino was even shorter than he'd thought, and the uniform of a four-star general smelled heavily of marijuana. He managed to try on a greasy Stetson with Gary Cooper's name stenciled on the sweatband before a small woman with a thimble on one thumb snatched it off his head and returned it to its place on a shelf lined with heads made of Styrofoam.

"Go to Grauman's and try your feet in his prints," she said. "This is a place of work."

"Sorry."

"What did you do, wander away from the group?"

"I'm an archivist, not a tourist."

"Is your name Gary Cooper?"

"No. It's Valentino."

She charged off, speaking in rapid Polish.

After that his interest waned. It was just a warehouse after all. He was circling the room aimlessly, trying to stay out of the way of thundering racks on wheels and personnel darting about with hat pins and giant shears, when Broadhead caught his eye and waved him over to where he and Sister Agnes were standing. Fanta was nowhere in sight.

As Valentino approached, a handsome black woman dressed in a smock similar to the costume technician's unloaded a pile of clothing onto Agnes' cutting table. The woman in charge scooped a military shako off the top of the pile and stuck it on his head.

It was two sizes too large. When he raised it to clear his vision, she was holding a matching tunic up in front of him, pressing the shoulders against his at arm's length to judge the effect. "It needs to be let out a little at the waist," she said. "They wore corsets then. Unless . . . ?" She lifted penciled brows above her glasses.

"No corset," Broadhead said. "Anyway, he looks like he's in a marching band."

She threw the tunic next to the pile and

snatched away the shako as he was taking it off. They were hard on hats there, and even harder on humans.

Broadhead said, "No uniforms. That's just a little too on the money. The old guy's senile, not stupid. What else have you got?"

Valentino said, "Just what —"

Fanta glided up to the table, shoulders bare above a lace bodice and lifting pounds of skirts and petticoats clear of the floor. She was beaming. "Michelle Pfeiffer and I wear the same size." She turned a malicious glance on Sister Agnes. "Two."

A young man came hurrying up behind her with a tape measure draped around his neck, looking nervous.

Sister Agnes fixed him with a cold stare. "That dress is on loan from Columbia. Is this how you impress pretty girls when I'm not around?"

"Uh, that isn't an issue," he said. "I mean, I'm sorry. She was so excited, and I saw you talking to her a few minutes ago, so I thought she was a VIP."

"You'll be DOA in Human Resources if you don't get it off her and back on the rack in five minutes. Unless you want to pay for it out of your salary."

"Yes, ma'am." He put a hand on Fanta's shoulder to steer her away.

"I didn't mean to get anyone in trouble," she said.

Valentino turned to Broadhead to intervene. The look on the professor's face startled him. All the muscles had gone slack, as if he'd suffered a seizure.

Broadhead said, "You look stunning."

Fanta eyed him closely, suspicion stamped on every feature. "You mean like something a Victorian threw up all over a wedding cake."

"No. Really beautiful. You should look like that more often. What I mean is, it wouldn't kill you to put on a dress now and then."

Sister Agnes cleared her throat loudly. Every sewing machine in the room stopped whirring. "Can we do this? I'm expecting a plague of Baldwins at six."

Fanta went away with the young man to change, stopping once to glance back at Broadhead. The sewing machines started back up.

"Sorry for the distraction." Broadhead pointed with unnecessary violence at the next item of apparel on the pile. He seemed to be skewering an invisible adversary. "Let's see that one."

It was a black swallowtail coat, intended to be worn with a shirt board and a low-cut formal vest. Those items and a pair of gray striped trousers lay next on the stack.

Broadhead vetoed the coat as Sister Agnes was trying it on Valentino. "Too late in the day. What happened between them took place twenty-five years before *Sunset Boulevard.*"

At last the archivist realized what was going through his friend's mind. "This is harebrained," he said. "If I had any idea this is what you were hatching, I'd never have let you drag me down here."

"If I had any idea you would, I'd have told you what I was hatching. What the devil's this, another comic-opera uniform? Universal must be planning a full-scale adaptation of *H.M.S. Pinafore.*" He pawed down through the pile.

"It won't work."

"Someone is forced to say that in every screwball comedy, and of course it always does. Is this Harris tweed?" He held up a brown herringbone Norfolk jacket.

"Ray Milland wore it in *Bulldog Drummond Escapes,*" Sister Agnes said. "I wouldn't keep it on more than a couple of hours. It's been in mothballs so long it's probably toxic to the skin."

"A couple of hours should be more than enough." Broadhead held it up against Valentino. "Perfect, and that's as much praise as your physical charms will ever receive from me. Milland cut quite a figure in his day."

"I won't wear it."

"It'd be a crime not to, a fit like this. Von Stroheim couldn't decide whether he wanted to be a proper English country gentleman or Frederick the Great. Since walking shoes are more comfortable than jackboots, Brittania ruled. Try it on."

"No. It's a numbskull notion. What's more, it's sick. I didn't get into this profession to take advantage of an old man's illness no matter what he's done. And we don't know if he's done anything wrong."

"Of course not. If we did, you wouldn't have to play dress-up at all. Where's the changing room?"

"I'm not parading across L.A. in August dressed like I'm riding to hounds!"

"Why do you think I was happy it's raining?" He turned to Sister Agnes. "A yellow slicker would be peachy. One of those big loose ones like firemen wear."

She jerked her chin at the black woman, who went toward the stairs to the upper racks.

"Great. Now I'll look like a school bus."

"This isn't about you, or how you'll look to strangers," Broadhead said. "It's about

Greed."

Fanta, back in her tank top and cargo pants and transparent plastic raincoat, returned while they were arguing, listened for a minute, and said, "You know you're going to do it, so why don't you save your voice? You'll need it to carry off the accent."

"You approve?" he said. "Of course you do, what was I thinking? You're our resident expert on civil disobedience. How do you keep your grades in ethics courses from dragging down your average?"

"I passed with a term paper on conscience. Mine's clear. I'm not the one who's haunted."

"I'm not haunted."

"Sure you are. You don't need chains and a creepy old house to qualify."

Valentino fumed, Broadhead purred, Fanta reasoned, Sister Agnes sighed and tapped her foot, and in the end her assistant escorted Valentino to a changing room behind a heavy curtain. Ten minutes later he exhibited himself to the others in a tweed suit that fit him loosely in the shoulders but snugly everywhere else, with a knitted tie on a soft Oxford shirt. He carried his street clothes in a bundle under one arm. The fumes from the mothballs forced him to hold his chin high to keep his eyes from watering; Broadhead said the pose enhanced the illusion of Erich von Stroheim at the arrogant peak of his powers.

Fanta agreed. "You don't look like the same man."

"I'm not. I'm a walking dress dummy. My skin itches all over. I think the poison's working."

Broadhead said, "Save some drama for opening night. You're probably just allergic to wool." He squinted. "Something's wrong."

"You're just realizing that?"

"He has too much hair," Sister Agnes said.

"That's it. Von Stroheim was bald."

"I'm not shaving my head!"

The professor took off his bucket hat, turned the brim up in back in a Tyrolean effect, and placed it on Valentino's head at a rakish angle. Then he stepped back to take in the whole picture. "With a stick and a monocle, and if you remember to stand with your back to the light, it might not be a disaster. It'll help if the old fellow has cataracts."

"He hasn't," Valentino said. "His eyes are fine and so's his hearing. I'm beginning to worry about yours."

"The stick we can do," Sister Agnes said. "No monocle. That's the prop department."

Broadhead said, "A stick's a prop."

"It's contractual. My predecessor lived through the Great Falsie Strike: Wardrobe and makeup both claimed jurisdiction over bra pads. The unions ironed it out by assigning the rubber ones to makeup and the cotton ones to wardrobe." She peered down at her watch.

"Von Stroheim's not von Stroheim without his monocle," Broadhead said. "I don't know anyone in the prop department."

Sister Agnes sighed. She took off her glasses and pressed at one of the round thick lenses with a thumb until something popped. She put the glasses back on and held the loose lens out to Valentino, shutting her naked eye. "Take care of it. Someone else will have to thread all my needles until you bring it back."

CHAPTER 21

"Stop squirming," Broadhead said.

"I can't help it," said Valentino. "This suit's scratching me to death. I'm breaking out in a rash."

"Can you two hold it down?" Fanta, behind the wheel, glared at them in the rearview mirror. "This car's bigger than my roommate's. It's hard enough steering it through traffic without you weirding out in the backseat."

Broadhead thrust the makeshift monocle into Valentino's hand. "Practice with this. It'll take your mind off the itching."

It wasn't just the suit that bothered him, or even the oppressive stench of camphor from the mothballs, which had forced Fanta to open all four windows to prevent asphyxiation, letting in rain. The bulky yellow oilcloth slicker he wore to cover his disguise was stifling. The heat increased perspiration, which aggravated the abrasion. He accepted the distraction of the monocle and tried fitting it to his left eye. It kept popping out.

"Try the right," Broadhead said. "That was where von Stroheim wore it anyway."

"That's my dominant eye. I can't see a thing through this lens. It'll be tough enough convincing him I'm an immortal director without bumping into walls."

"Well, keep practicing. If a kid can balance a spoon on the end of his nose, you can keep a hunk of glass in your eye."

Fanta said, "I've got Crazy Glue in my bag."

Valentino redoubled his efforts. Eventually he screwed it into a position where the muscles held it in place.

"Let's hear the accent."

"Achtung! Gesundheit! Sauerbraten!"

"That's Chaplin. *The Great Dictator.* More Bavaria, less Birkenwald. And spare us the sum total of your German. Pegler's wife's name was Gerda. He may know more than you do."

"Varren? Varren Peckler, is dat choo?"

Silence filled the car, surrounded by honking horns and the rumble of a motorcycle.

"Dr. Zinnerman was wrong," Fanta said. "I'm not the worst actor who ever lived."

"I never claimed to be any other kind."

His cheeks burned, as if the rash were spreading.

But Broadhead was sanguine. "Even the best talents need direction. Try again. You're a foreigner trying to sound like an American, not the other way around."

"Varren Pegler, is dat choo?"

"Better."

Fanta said, "It sounded the same."

"No, this time I heard the *g,* and the *V* was softer."

Valentino said, "I sounded like a Katzenjammer Kid even to me."

"You're not directing this performance. Try something else, this time with a soupçon of German."

"I vant *mein Kindling!*"

"That was Garbo."

"I'm quoting von Stroheim directly. From my dream, I mean."

"Well, I wish you'd bring him back. It may take the greatest auteur of the last century to carry this one off."

"I told you it was hopeless."

"Try it again, without the firewood."

"*Kindling* isn't —"

"It sounds like it when you say it. Say, 'I want *Greed.*"

"I vant *Greed!*"

"Give me the *w.*"

"I want *Greed*!"

"Drop the exclamation point."

"I want *Greed*."

Broadhead looked up at the rearview mirror. Valentino saw his satisfaction reflected in Fanta's eyes.

Broadhead said, "By George —"

"Stop right there," Valentino said. "Before you break into a number."

"Now shout it."

"I want *Greed*!"

"Without the exclamation point, I said."

"How can you shout without exclaiming?"

"Ask yourself that question. You're von Stroheim."

"*I want* Greed."

"Again."

"*I want* Greed."

"Once more. You're angry, but you're desperate. You're demanding and pleading at the same time."

"*I want* Greed."

This time it rang off the headliner, tearing something loose inside him and numbing him to his fingers and toes. Belatedly he realized they'd stopped for a red light. The Mexican cab driver stopped next to them turned away from the holy icons stuck to his dash to stare at the red-faced man in the Tyrolean hat and yellow slicker. Valentino raised a sheepish hand. The driver shifted his attention to the truck in front of him without returning the wave.

"Congratulations," Broadhead said. "That's your first rave review."

"I'm sure he doesn't think he's the one who was raving."

"He must be new to Los Angeles," Fanta said.

The light changed. They resumed moving. Valentino retrieved his monocle from his lap and returned it to where it had popped loose. "Give me something else."

Fanta said, "Do 'Show me the money!' "

"That's the spirit, both of you." Broadhead chuckled. "Sorry. I meant 'enthusiasm.' "

When Valentino ran out of lines and started quoting from *Hogan's Heroes,* he began to get hammy again. Broadhead told him to rest his voice.

"I keep thinking about those reels," he said as they entered the Santa Monica Freeway. "Not so much why they were divided between the projection booth and the basement, but where. The four-hour cut Thalberg released originally ran twenty-four reels. That was exactly as many as there were in the booth."

Valentino sat up. "Do you think it isn't a

complete print?"

"No. Twenty-five picks up where twenty-four left off, long before Pitts's murder. I couldn't resist peeking. It's just a strange coincidence that whoever went out of his way to store the rest in the basement should choose the very reels that would indicate it ran the full eight hours."

"Or ten," Fanta said. "I wonder if we'll ever know for sure just how long it is."

"We may, if Val doesn't forget himself and start channeling Colonel Klink."

A familiar tune played inside the car. Valentino fumbled at his pockets, then remembered his street clothes in the bundle on the front passenger's seat. "That's my cell."

Fanta found it and handed it to him over the back of the seat.

Broadhead said, "You downloaded the theme to *Gone With the Wind*?"

"The soundtrack selection was thin." He looked at the LED. "It's Sergeant Clifford's number in West Hollywood." He tugged up the antenna.

The professor tore the phone out of his hand and threw it out the window. A car coming up on the outside lane chirped its brakes and swerved to avoid the unidentified flying object. Fanta took evasive measures, cutting off a minivan on the inside and starting a chain reaction of screeching brakes and furious horns.

Valentino stared at Broadhead. "That was unexpected."

"Yes, she's a more accomplished driver than I thought."

"Kyle, I have a stick." He lifted the malacca cane by its crook. The tag tied to it with string read PROPERTY OF UNIVERSAL PICTURES.

"These days the police can trace you through your cell phone signal," Broadhead said. "I doubt they'd offer us an escort to the Country Home."

"We don't know that was a hostile call."

"Have you ever received any other kind from that number?"

"It's early for them to have made it past those first three reels of film. Especially if they're examining it frame by frame."

"Unlike archivists and academics, not all cops are obsessive-compulsive. They might be perverse enough to inspect them out of order. I barely had time to change the labels on the cans, and none at all to edit out the title sequences."

"So now we're fugitives from justice."

"I prefer to think of it as 'fugitives *for* justice.' I'm beginning to believe that Rin-

Tin-Tin was an appropriate choice."

"Stop the car," Valentino told Fanta.

She met his gaze in the mirror. "In the middle of the Santa Monica Freeway?"

"Find an exit with a telephone. It's not always easy to tell when things have gone too far, but when you're running away from the law dressed like a dead Austrian movie director, it's clear you've crossed the line."

"All the more reason to keep going," Broadhead said.

"That's what Bonnie told Clyde."

"If she hadn't, the movie would have been shorter, but the ending wouldn't have changed. This isn't George Washington and the cherry tree. Clifford won't reward your honesty by returning the film. She'll hang it up that much longer to use as evidence in our prosecution, and this time she won't be disposed to observe the niceties of cold storage. We passed the point of no return the moment you put on that monocle."

"Believe it or not, there are more important things than rescuing a movie. Fanta belongs in that category. How's she going to practice law with a felony on her record?"

"She's a minor. I'll say I took her hostage."

She spoke up. "That's bogus. I turn twenty-one next month. I'm old enough to know what I'm getting into."

"Then you must be older than I am," Valentino said. "At least I've got a good chance of pleading insanity in this outfit."

Broadhead said, "We're already turning on each other, and we're not even in custody yet. Whatever happened to honor among thieves?"

Valentino started laughing.

He laughed so hard the monocle flew out of his eye and landed somewhere on the floor. Tears formed and he hiked up the sleeve of his slicker and dragged a tweed cuff across his eyes. "Ouch. What'd they weave this from, barbed wire?"

That brought on a new fit. His chest ached and his throat was raw, a symptom of his allergy to wool and the harsh German gutturals that had rasped through it. Bad acting was funny. He guffawed. When at last he grew too exhausted to raise even a giggle, he realized they were no longer moving. Fanta had pulled off onto the shoulder of the exit to Woodland Hills and sat with one elbow over the back of the seat, watching him with brow puckered. He was aware too of Broadhead's scrutiny.

"A little hysteria is refreshing," his friend said then. "Cracking apart like Bette Davis on the stand is a tad over the top."

"I'm not crazy." Valentino caught his

breath. His side hurt. "I thought I was all week, but I know now I'm the only sane member of the cast. Every good Mack Sennett short needs a straight man. Anytime now I expect to look out the back window and see an army of cops with clubs and Chester Conklin moustaches swarming up from the Valley."

Broadhead rumpled his hair. "You never called Kym Trujillo in Admissions. Why don't we find a phone, and if she says it isn't a good time to visit Pegler, we'll go home. This may not be your night to perform."

"It's my only night. Help me find Sister Agnes' right eye, will you? I think it rolled under Fanta's seat."

The professor found it and wiped it on his trousers. He examined both sides. "You were right. This wouldn't fool a baby."

"Babies are easier to fool than Clifford. If her people haven't spotted the switch by now, they're sure to before we get another chance. They won't stop to listen to our theories while they're booking us." He took the monocle and stuck it in his eye socket. "I may be going out there a kid from the chorus, but I've got to come back a star."

"Ew," Fanta said.

CHAPTER 22

No one stopped them to ask for ID on their way through the Motion Picture Country Home. There were no passes, no barred doors, no visible security personnel. In the huge foyer, a three-time Oscar nominee for Best Original Soundtrack played "Chopsticks" on a white baby grand that had once belonged to George Gershwin. His fingering was flawless.

"All these famous old people," said Fanta. "Aren't they at risk too?"

Broadhead grunted. "Not as much as Charlize Theron's underwear at Universal. This town has the long-term memory of a fruit fly."

Valentino demurred. He crowded close to his companions, self-conscious of his over-size slicker and walking stick. He'd rolled the hat into a tube and put it in a slash pocket. "No other business in the world treats its veterans so well. In Russia they'd be shot the moment they had trouble remembering their lines."

"Not always a bad policy," Broadhead said. "It would have spared us Brando in *Last Tango.*"

The chubby young man was not at the desk in the office. Behind the trivet that read ASSISTANT ACTIVITIES DIRECTOR sat an equally heavyset young woman in a USC sweatshirt, and her differing approach to the work showed in the rubble that had already accumulated on the glass desktop. Paperwork, loose-leaf fillers filled with loose leaves, and boxes and boxes of board games built a retaining wall with TRIVIAL PURSUIT: MOVIE EDITION balanced on top.

Broadhead pointed to the last. "That must end in a bloody draw every time."

She made no response. The stockade of clutter seemed to represent a shield between her and the professor's disarming brand of charm. She held up a sheet of names she'd managed to extract from the pile. "You're not on the list. I'll need to check with Ms. Trujillo." She launched an expedition for the telephone.

"We'll wait." He looked around for a seat.

"Visitor's room's down the hall on the left."

This was a well-lighted area with

comfortable-looking chairs and sofas and a plasma TV, before which crouched a couple of former character actors with hearing aids, shouting answers at the screen. The plastic sleeve on the coffee table identified the game they were playing as Scene It?, an interactive DVD about the history of film.

"Allen Jenkins!" cried one.

"Roscoe Karns, you idiot," said the other.

The answer was Joe Sawyer.

"Who in thunder's Joe Sawyer?" asked the first.

"Not Allen Jenkins, that's for sure."

"You thought he was Roscoe Karns."

"I did not."

"You said Roscoe Karns."

"Your battery's dead."

"You'd think they'd know more," Broadhead muttered.

Valentino approached a familiar figure reading a tattered script by the rain-streaked window, a slender man in his sixties in slacks and a pullover sweater with a silk scarf knotted around his throat. He'd played a juvenile well into his forties, and nothing since he'd begun to show his age. He smiled when he recognized Valentino and shook his hand without getting up.

"How are you?" asked the visitor.

"If you'd asked me last week, I'd have had

to say not so good." He slapped the script. "They're remaking the first thing I ever got credit for, over at Fox. This time they want me to read for the character's grandfather. Rob Reiner's directing."

"Congratulations."

"There might be a nomination in it. Look at Gloria Stuart."

Valentino introduced Broadhead and Fanta. They chatted, wished him luck, and drifted away as he returned to his lines.

"That's cool," Fanta said.

Valentino said, "Don't believe everything you hear under this roof. There's usually a man behind the curtain."

Broadhead said, "Did you see how old that script was?"

"It's probably the same one he had when he was seventeen."

"You mean he dreamed up the audition? That's whack."

"Oh, some assistant at Fox might have made a courtesy call, but that's probably the end of it," Valentino said. "His last chance for a comeback blew up when some sleaze journalist outed him on the set of *The Edge of Night.* The blacklist never really went away; it just changes its targets with the fashion."

"But it's okay to be gay now," she said.

"It wasn't then. In the end all they remember is you're some kind of damaged goods."

"But no other business in the world treats its veterans so well," said Broadhead.

"I said it didn't shoot them. Everyone's afraid of losing the job he's got."

Kym Trujillo joined them, carrying file folders as usual. She acknowledged Valentino's introductions with a preoccupied air.

"You usually call," she said.

"I meant to, but I lost my cell phone."

She noticed the slicker. "Are you expecting a hurricane?"

"I may be coming down with a cold."

"Where's your straw hat?" She pointed at the cane with the corner of a folder.

"I threw my back out."

She freed a hand to reach down and turn the paper tag so she could read it.

"I threw it out at Universal," he said.

"You're just falling apart, aren't you? Should I get a room ready?"

"I take back what I said before," Broadhead said. "I'm not your only friend."

"Is Warren Pegler in his room?" Valentino asked.

"I saw his nurse going into the break room. I'll check. It's not as if I have a department to run or anything like that." She strode out the door.

"Attractive woman," Broadhead said.

"Tough customer," said Fanta. "What did you say her name was?"

"Greer Garson!"

This was one of the game players huddled in front of the TV.

"It's Shelley Winters, you moron," said the other. "Don't you know the difference between Mrs. Miniver and Lolita?"

"Shelley Winters wasn't Lolita. That was Sandra Dee."

"Sandra Dee was Gidget."

"Then who in thunder was Lolita?"

"Search me, but it sure wasn't Greer Garson."

"I didn't say it was."

"Did too."

"Didn't."

Broadhead said, "I'd swear I was at a meeting of the university faculty."

"You haven't been to one in years," Valentino said.

"I wonder why," Fanta said.

Kym returned, worry lines on her forehead. "He's in the solarium, with an attendant. He's not having a good day. I wish you'd called. In his condition he's easily agitated."

"A little agitation might do him some good," Broadhead suggested. "Increase the blood flow to his brain."

She asked him if he was a medical doctor.

He shook his head. "History and Humanities. I can prescribe a course of study, but that's all."

"Alzheimer's is different from simple senility," she said. "Accelerated circulation can trigger paranoia, even violence. I'm not his physician, so I can't forbid you to see him if he himself doesn't object, but I don't think a visit would do you or him any good in this mood."

Valentino said, "There's a time factor involved. I don't mean to be cold-blooded, but at his age I don't know how many other chances we'll have to get answers to the questions we need to ask. Primary sources are crucial."

Her expression was unreadable, which he regarded as a bad sign.

"Unfortunately — fortunately, for you — his doctor is in Cedars of Lebanon this afternoon, attending a patient from this facility. If he were present, I doubt he'd let you see Warren. But our policy is to respect the resident's wishes in the absence of medical opinion. I'll take you to him, but I need to ask him if he'll see you. If he says no, that's it."

Valentino started to thank her.

"Thank the patients' bill of rights. This is the first time I've known you to put your job ahead of respect for your sources."

"This is the first time it's been this important."

She made a slashing gesture with her free hand, severing the discussion. He hoped that was all she'd severed. She turned and broke into a trot. The three followed.

"*Ben-Hur!*"

"*The Ten Commandments,* you jerk. You can't even keep your Testaments straight."

On his way past the two old character actors, Broadhead stopped to snatch the remote out of the hand holding it, pointed it at the plasma screen, and pushed a button. The screen went black. He smacked the remote down on the coffee table. "Isn't there a game of checkers going on in the park?"

The pale, seamed, half-remembered faces stared up at him with injury and indignation.

"It's raining," one said.

In the hallway, Valentino asked Broadhead what he thought he'd accomplished.

"Nothing. I saw myself in ten years."

Fanta said, "I know the pictures they were talking about."

"Forget them," Broadhead said. "Erase

them from your memory. Consider it a step back from the graveyard. The only thing a girl your age should know about is who's in Air Supply."

"Air Supply was my mother's favorite."

He groaned mortally.

The sun's access to the solarium was limited that day. The room was in effect a greenhouse, built of glass on a steel frame, with palms and ferns growing in profusion from terra-cotta pots and wicker and rattan all around. But the look that afternoon was film *gris.* The persistent rain bled viscuously down the panes, blurring the vista of cul-de-sacs and feral palms and third-generation Spanish Modern housing developments stacked one atop another to the scrub hills and the towering wooden letters of the fabled Hollywood sign staggered across them. It looked like the phoniest process shot from a film made entirely on a sound-stage in Cincinnati. Valentino, Broadhead, and Fanta hung back in the wide sliding-glass doorway while Kym conferred with a blocky attendant in casual dress and the man in the wheelchair at the far end of the room. The three were dwarfed by scenery that Valentino felt would shoot up onto a roller, flapping comically, the moment someone tugged on a cord.

They were alone in the room, despite abundant seating. A cheerful place when the sun shone, it now wore a sodden air of bleak introspection, with each drop that plunked from a leaky gutter measuring the passage of time like a tick from a clock.

The man in the wheelchair turned his head to look at the visitors. Valentino recognized the white hair and withered face. At that distance he couldn't tell if the recognition was mutual. The old man turned back, raised a hand from the arm of the chair, and let it drop. Kym strode back their way, her spine as straight as in her days on the runway.

"Twenty minutes, with the attendant present," she said. "If Warren becomes upset, he'll shut you down."

"We'll be careful," Valentino said.

She left without another word.

Broadhead stopped him before he could take a step inside. The professor reached down and jerked loose the wardrobe-department tag from his walking stick. "No reshoots on this set," he said. "You've got to get it right on the first take."

Valentino thrust the stick at him and held it until Broadhead took it. Then he fastened the snaps on the slicker to the neck, concealing completely what he wore beneath. "Let's give honesty a chance. If it doesn't work, we'll try it your way."

"I'll distract the guard." Broadhead spoke out of the side of his mouth.

"Let me." Fanta wound an arm inside his, as she had once before with Valentino. "Lean on that cane, and follow my lead."

The attendant was fortyish, powerfully built, with broad, honest features, a receding hairline, and a plastic badge on his shirt that said his name was Todd. His expression was polite but wary.

Fanta gave him her best coed's smile. "Todd, I wonder if my grandfather and I can ask you a few questions about the Country Home. He's considering moving in." She patted Broadhead's arm.

"You should talk to Ms. Trujillo." Todd had a rough, burring voice, accustomed to intimidating belligerent patients. "I can't show you around. I have to stay here with Warren."

"Oh, we won't have to leave the room. We just want the perspective of someone who spends most of his time with the residents. Grandpa's particular. He produced *Dallas*."

"*Masterpiece Theater*," Broadhead corrected. "I became a father at a very young age. Most people think Frances is my daughter."

"Well, I've been here a year. I guess I could fill you in."

They drifted down the room, Broadhead supporting himself on the cane and Fanta's arm, Todd stooping a little to talk and listen with his hands folded behind his back. Valentino smiled down at Warren Pegler. "Hello," he said. "Do you remember me?"

Pegler looked up, squinting. "Erich, that you?"

CHAPTER 23

Valentino hesitated. He'd actually heard the *h* in Erich. The old man's eyes, normally as sharp and bright as a bird's, were smoky. He was wearing another crisp dress shirt, fresh trousers stitched neatly at the knees where his legs ended, but today he seemed shrunken inside his clothes. His complexion was as gray as the scene outside the glass.

Valentino was tempted. But he chose the high road.

"We met the other day. I asked you some things about the Oracle theater."

"That money hole." The eyes cleared. "The miserable place took everything I had."

"You put a lot into it: widescreen technology, three-D projectors, new speakers for stereo. That must have cost a bundle. Did you take out a loan?"

"Stole it."

Valentino's face went numb.

"Tax man, building inspectors, my business manager — hell, even my employees. They stole the place right out from under me, just as if they'd used a gun."

The visitor relaxed. He drew up a wicker armchair and sat on the edge facing Pegler. "I was curious about that. You said your business manager took your investments and disappeared into Nazi Germany."

"He was a friend of Gerda's family. They all came over on the same boat. But a Kraut's a Kraut. He took my whole portfolio and gave it to Hitler for a good spot in the Party. Gerda's half Swiss, that's her saving grace." He'd switched tenses again. The past seemed to move in and out of focus without warning.

"That must have been before the war ended in forty-five. You hung on to the theater another eleven years. How'd you pay for all those improvements?"

The old man stared at something above Valentino's head, possibly old ghosts. "Pipe that, will you? This is the only place in the world where they need a big sign to tell them where they live." He was looking at the Hollywood sign.

Valentino tried it again from a different angle. "Albert Spinoza. Did he work for you? He was a projectionist."

"I'm sorry, son. Who'd you say you were?"

He sighed and told him his name.

"No, it isn't. I'm not that far gone. He died way back when I was in physical therapy."

"Tell me about the accident at Metro."

"Some damn fool left a cigarette burning next to fresh film stock. When the flames hit the chemicals on the shelves, the darkroom went up and me with it. They had to cut me in half to save what didn't burn." He rubbed one of his stumps.

"You almost died in the fire. You would have, if Erich von Stroheim hadn't been nearby."

"That fraud. *Von* Stroheim, my aunt's fanny. I bet he shoveled out the stables."

"What about recreation?" Fanta was asking the attendant at the other end of the room. "I don't want Grandpa just sitting around watching Nick at Nite like he does at home."

"The Discovery Channel," Broadhead corrected.

Valentino leaned closer. "Spinoza was a runaway. He might have been using a different name. Twenty-one years old, short, slightly built. He disappeared not too long before you sold the theater."

The eyes in the pleated face grew sharp as

points of crystal. If the visitor had been looking away he'd have missed it, because in the next instant they went as dull as if his brain had cast over.

"I didn't catch your name," Pegler said. "Did you say Mr. Thalberg sent you?"

Valentino searched his face. He couldn't tell if it was an act. He glanced toward the others. Todd was pointing something out on a floor plan of the facility mounted on the solid wall beside the entrance. Fanta was asking a question. Broadhead turned his head, catching Valentino's eye.

Showtime.

"Excuse me," he said, unnecessarily; Pegler appeared to have forgotten he was there. He got up, stepped around behind the wheelchair, and shed the yellow slicker onto a rattan love seat, retrieving the soft hat from the pocket. He put it on at an arrogant angle with the brim turned up in back, the front turned down over one side of his forehead. He adjusted the tweed coat, tightened his tie, took the naked lens from a watch pocket, blew lint off it, and screwed it into his right eye. He missed the cane, but it was proving useful elsewhere. He squared his shoulders, lifted his chin, and stamped his feet around in a brisk half circle, finishing with his back to the window, glaring down at the old man with the light coming from behind him.

"Varren?" He paused to soften the accent slightly. "Warren Pegler, is that you?"

Pegler's face lifted slowly as dawn. Confusion rippled across the features, then spread out smooth. A sardonic smile twisted the cracked lips.

"Erich, you old fake. Still wearing that monocle. I bet you're blind in both eyes by now. Someone told me you were dying."

Valentino held his breath. Von Stroheim had died in France in 1957, six months after Pegler sold The Oracle. He'd been dying when Albert Spinoza disappeared.

He willed himself to stay in character. "I am not dead yet, you drugstore developer. Where is *mein Kindling?*"

"Speak English, you damn Kraut. Over here we burn kindling. Burning, that's something you know a little bit about."

That almost shook him out of his role. This was territory he hadn't covered.

"*I want* Greed," he said.

It came out louder than intended. Startled, Todd looked their way. Fanta repositioned herself in front of him and raised her voice to ask if the swimming pool was heated. Valentino took in his breath again, let it out when the attendant cleared his throat and explained that there was a heated pool outdoors and an unheated one in the recreation room.

Pegler looked befuddled. Valentino pressed his advantage. "Don't act stupid." *Schtupid* came out in a harsh whisper. "You developed every frame of the original forty-two reels. I know you didn't destroy them when T'alberg ordered you to. I want *Greed*!"

The man in the wheelchair flinched, as if he'd shouted again. For the first time he seemed afraid; his jaw wobbled. Valentino felt sick to his stomach. Bullying a weak old man hadn't been part of the plan.

"Who told you there were forty-two reels? I only showed you twenty-four. Have you been talking to Spinoza?"

His visitor felt hot all over. It had nothing to do with wearing heavy wool in California in August.

The twisted smile returned. Pegler's eyes were clear again, but glassy. He was seeing the past with a clarity of vision mere memory could not provide. "Well, no matter. I was saving the rest to bleed you later, when you thought you'd bought me off for good. I had Gerda hide the rest of the reels in the basement for the second show. It's all here in the theater, every last sweaty, self-indulgent inch of your damn masterpiece, and you'll keep on paying me storage till I get sick of looking at them and sell them to you outright. And if you stop paying, or hire some studio thug to break in and steal them, I'll put a match to them, even if it means burning the miserable building to the ground and me with it. It won't take long. You've seen yourself how fast that stuff goes up." He was stroking both his stumps with his hands.

"You are blackmailing me?" It came out *blackmailink,* but without self-conscious burlesque. He *was* von Stroheim. He raised his imaginary stick. Now it was a riding crop poised to strike an insubordinate junior officer. "I saved your life!"

" 'I saffed your life!' " Pegler mocked the accent. "Gerda's been in this country nowhere near as long as you, and she speaks the language better. You don't know where all those cheesy parts leave off and you begin. Okay, you saffed my liffe. You wouldn't have had to *saffe* it at all if you hadn't put it in danger in the first place. Why didn't you save my legs while you were at it?"

The old man's voice was shrill. Todd took a step their way.

Fanta put a hand on his arm. "Let me talk to my brother. He gets carried away sometimes." Over her shoulder she said, "Grandpa, ask him about the library. You know how much you love westerns."

"Western philosophy," Broadhead corrected. "Let's get down to brass tacks. Tell me, young man, are there any attractive widows in residence?"

The fit of emotion had subsided. The old man sat as calmly as if it had never taken place. Valentino sank down onto the chair facing him. His own legs were rubbery. The attendant frowned, then rolled his great shoulders and turned back to answer Broadhead's question.

"Everything all right?" Fanta's tone was soothing.

Valentino, rattled and forgetting his role, started to answer.

Pegler interrupted him. He looked up at the young woman with an expression so nakedly guilty he shared the old man's discomfort. "Gerda. I thought you were downstairs in the auditorium."

She and Valentino exchanged glances. He nodded.

She straightened her posture and folded her hands at her waist. "I heard a noise and came up." Her speech was slower than normal, the tone deeper. "Warren, what have you done?"

He jerked his chin toward the floor. "I caught this young fool going through storage. I told him to stay out of there and in the booth where he belongs, but he got nosy. He must have heard about *Greed* at that theater he worked in back East. I couldn't have him running around telling everyone he found it. I hit him with an empty can. Might as well throw it away, it's too bent up to use. Do you think he's dead?"

The silence was complete. Even Todd and Broadhead had stopped talking and were watching them, motionless. They'd overheard.

Fanta shuddered. Valentino couldn't tell if it was real or if her drama teacher had grossly underestimated her talent. In that same slow, heavy speech she said, "His head's cracked open. What should we do?"

She'd lost the gamble. The eyes changed again, glittered lucidly. He seemed to be returning to the present. Then they clouded again.

"Gerda!"

The shout jarred the listeners. It was loud enough to carry all through the building. Pegler braced his hands on the arms of the wheelchair and raised himself from the seat, turning his head to call over his shoulder. "Gerda! You didn't finish that wall yet, did you? You forgot the reels in the storeroom. Come and get them."

In a minute or so they would be up to their necks in personnel. Everyone leaned forward, straining for what came next.

Pegler appeared to be listening to something, a voice dead to everyone but him. His arms went slack. He slumped back into the chair with his chin on his chest, a man much older than just ninety-eight. "No, leave the bricks up." His voice bleated weakly. "We'll just plaster it over. Von Stroheim's dying. We won't be getting any more money out of him. We'll just go ahead and sell the place."

"I am not dead yet."

The part of Valentino that was Valentino was chilled by the voice that broke the stillness; it might have belonged to von Stroheim's ghost and not himself. He wasn't in control of it. Valentino held up a hand to stop the stampede of rescuers at the entrance to the room, Kym Trujillo at its head. Von Stroheim lowered it and gripped the arms of his chair as if it were the throne of Austria. All eyes were upon him.

"What did you mean when you said I put your life in danger?"

The thin old face stared back. It seemed to have been carved from petrified wood.

Then it bent in the middle, making a smile as sharp as a lance. "Still smoking, Erich?" he asked.

CHAPTER 24

The interview setup at police headquarters bore a certain resemblance to the layout of a psychiatrist's office, which seemed appropriate, given its location in downtown Los Angeles.

The waiting area was less comfortable, consisting of a row of hard chairs in a hallway, and in place of the usual outdated magazines the reading material was restricted to a display of posters on the glass wall opposite promoting safety; but the exit from interrogation was separate from the entrance, so that once a subject was called inside, he was not seen again by his fellows except on the other side of the glass on the way to the elevator. Valentino suspected that in the present case the arrangement had less to do with polite discretion than with preventing interviewees from comparing their stories.

He sat there for what seemed hours and

probably was; no clock was visible and he'd left his wristwatch in a pocket of his street clothes in the name of consistency of character. He was too tired to speculate with his neighbors. Kyle Broadhead and then Todd the attendant and then Fanta and finally Kym Trujillo were collected and escorted around the corner by an officer in uniform, to reappear briefly twenty or thirty minutes later, making their escape behind glass. There didn't seem to be any rhyme or reason to the order, like scenes shot out of context. Valentino was left alone. The air-conditioning in the hallway was inadequate, and although he'd shed the uncomfortable tweed jacket and hung it over the back of his chair, he was clammy with sweat and itched in patches big and small. His right eye kept twitching — payback from the muscles for subjecting them to a monocle, of all things. Peering through the thick prescription lens had given him a pounding headache. His back hurt and his neck was stiff. He wondered how von Stroheim had put up with it for seventy-one years. It seemed to explain his disposition.

Sergeant Clifford was letting him steep. He regarded that as just punishment. Sitting there marooned, he projected the events of the past week onto the glass wall in front of him and found himself picking holes in the plot. None of the motivations made sense, the characters kept second-guessing one another, and the hero appeared ridiculous. If he'd been in a theater, he'd have walked out soon after the opening credits.

"May I join you, or will you be brooding alone this evening?"

He looked up at Kym Trujillo, standing beside his chair with her hands in the pockets of a short silvery all-weather coat. Rain was still falling, or had been anyway the last time he'd seen the outdoors. He started to get up.

"Stay put. If you came to the Country Home looking like that, I'd order oxygen."

"How'd you make it back here?" he asked. "I saw you bolting for freedom a little while ago."

"I shook my tail and doubled back. Actually, they don't care what happens to you after you leave the place. They don't even offer you a ride home after they bring you here in the backseat of a squad car. I drove. Should I hang around?"

"You might have to wait one to three years. Whatever the going rate is for obstruction of justice."

She sat down in the chair next to him.

"You caught a murderer. That should count for something."

"I browbeat a confession out of an old man in a wheelchair."

"I've been in elder care five years," she said. "The woman I replaced was there when poor Johnny Weismuller started wandering into the other residents' rooms, giving the Tarzan yell. He won five gold medals in two Olympics, broke the world speed swimming record twice, and made twenty-seven movies, but at the home he's remembered as a pathetic old pest. It's easy to forget what they were when you see them as they are. Warren Pegler is an old man in a wheelchair who bludgeoned a man to death in the prime of his life. Also he's a blackmailer."

"Can we not talk about that?" he asked. "I betrayed your trust."

"I'll be a while forgiving you for that. Was it worth all the fuss?"

"I've been telling myself all along it was. Sitting here these last few hours, I'm not so sure. Kyle Broadhead says I can sell *Greed* to UCLA for fifty thousand. I've been wondering if that's what I went to all the fuss for, and all this high-minded talk of saving a great work of art is so much hooey. Maybe von Stroheim was right. Maybe it all comes down to greed in the end."

She was quiet for a minute.

"Maybe you're thinking too much about the end and not enough about the beginning," she said then. "Go back to the first time you visited that projection booth and read the labels on those cans. How'd you feel?"

"My palms got sweaty and my heart rate shot to two hundred."

"Was it like winning the lottery?"

"I've never won the lottery. I've never played."

"Well, was it like coming into unexpected money?"

"No. It was like what Hillary said when he climbed Everest. He couldn't wait to see the expression on the face of the leader of the expedition when he came back down. I couldn't wait to tell Kyle."

"That doesn't sound like the reaction of someone who just found the shortcut to Easy Street."

"It can't be as simple as that."

"Most things are, until you start picking at them. Why do you think they left us cooling our heels out here in the hallway?"

"So von Stroheim was wrong, and *Greed's* a fraud."

"It's a movie. If movies were real, there'd

be no reason to go to them." She yawned; he realized then she'd been up as long as he. "All I know is, someone who never played the lottery isn't in it for the money."

"Somehow I doubt Sergeant Clifford will be that charitable. How was it in there?"

"She's tough. She thought I was trying to make you look good because we're friends."

"We must be, if you were able to make me look good."

"I said I tried. Anyway, I only came in on the last act. I guess you'd call it the last reel. Todd would've given her the rest."

He looked at her out of the corner of his eye. "So are we friends?"

She kept her perfect profile turned his way. The modeling profession had lost a potential icon when she'd decided to go for an MBA. "Stay away from the Country Home for a while. The people I answer to don't read murder mysteries."

It was an unsatisfactory response, but he didn't push for more. He had neither the energy nor the moral authority.

The uniformed officer returned and scowled down at Kym. Valentino sensed in him a philosophical kinship with the stickler in the university parking garage. She rose to leave.

"The sergeant will see you now," he told

Valentino.

When Valentino stood and picked up the tweed jacket, Kym leaned over and kissed him on the cheek. "I'll send you a box of popcorn with a file in it," she whispered.

The interview room was nearly as clean as the lab, the linoleum tiles waxed recently and the walls glistening with fresh beige paint, but that was just cosmetics to cover a miasma of guilt and fear. Sergeant Clifford received him leaning in a corner with arms and ankles crossed. She wore a blue silk blouse and black slacks with an empty holster clipped to her belt. He didn't know if this was a precaution against attempts at escape or suicide or her own impatience. She looked taller than ever. Her mane of red hair was fiery in the light of a bare bulb in a cage on the ceiling. She told him to sit down.

"Not there. Face the mirror."

He draped the jacket over the back of a plastic scoop chair and sat at a laminated table. A video camera on a tripod regarded him with its unblinking red eye. His face in reflection looked wan and gray. He felt other eyes watching him from the opposite side of the glass.

"Tell it," she said.

He told it straight through, from his first

two visits to The Oracle and the discoveries he'd made there all the way through his second conversation with Warren Pegler that afternoon — yesterday afternoon, possibly; his inner clock insisted midnight was close, if not past. He went back a few times to provide details he'd forgotten, and terse questions from the sergeant reminded him of others. This time he didn't leave out Fanta and Broadhead and their contributions. He was sure *they* hadn't, and for once he'd decided that telling the whole truth would spare them further trouble. Then the questioning began in earnest and he told it all two or three more times, out of order. It was like cutting up a reel of film and having to splice it back together several times before he got it right. She was trying to trip him up, and she was good at her job. He found himself second-guessing things he'd been sure of all along and dismissing things he'd questioned earlier out of hand.

Finally the cross-examination stopped. For the first time in an hour she stirred herself from her corner, walked over to the camera, and pushed a button. The red light went off.

"I had a warrant all sworn out for your arrest when we got the call from Woodland Hills," she said, pulling out a chair and sitting down across from him. She folded her forearms on the table. "Did you think cops are too dumb to read title frames on film?"

He was still trying to construct an answer that wouldn't get him in deeper when she spoke again.

"Your friend Dr. Broadhead confessed to switching movies. He said you had nothing to do with it. I thought he was just protecting you, but I see now you're not culpable. Just stupid.

"As for interfering with an official police investigation," she went on, "you're guilty as Cain. You need to read something in the paper besides the entertainment section. The century turned a few years ago. These days, Sherlock Holmes would be spending so much time as a guest of Scotland Yard he wouldn't have any left to trample over footprints and taint evidence. Did you ever have one moment of madness where you thought it might be a good idea to call a professional and tell her what you'd stepped in?"

"I was pretty sure you'd tell me to butt out."

She stuck a red-nailed finger at him. "That's at the top of the list of One Hundred Reasons Why I'm a Detective and You're Not. I act on tips, no matter how looney the source. How'd you identify Albert Spinoza as the victim?"

"It's in my statement. Several places."

"Pretend it isn't."

"Fanta found an old newspaper article on the Internet. Everything about the missing person checked with what we knew about the skeleton." She was torturing him.

"What *we* knew; but that was public record, so I won't be calling Harriet Johansen up for a disciplinary hearing for spilling it to her gentleman friend. Here's another juicy piece of inside information: We have computers too. We were gathering more background to spring on Pegler when you and Mickey and Judy decided to put on a show. With it, we'd have gotten everything we needed from Pegler without blowing our case on a charge of entrapment."

He sat back as if she'd struck him across the face. "I never realized — I didn't think —"

"Bam!" An open hand smacked the table. "You Didn't Think. That's reason number two."

"Sergeant," he said, "I'm sorry. It was an old case, not exactly a priority with so many new ones coming across your desk every day. I was concerned with what might happen to *Greed* while it was simmering on the back burner. Do you really think Pegler will get away with it?"

"He already has. We haven't spoken with his physician yet, but based on the statements we took from the two Country Home employees who were present, the DA informs me no psychiatrist in the system will declare him fit to stand trial. At his age and in his condition, he'll probably never live long enough to be committed to an institution. Anyway, what's the point? He's in an institution now."

"Why do you think he did it?"

She sat back and crossed one leg over the other. Her eyes were smoky green. "He told you his fears. Delusional people don't lie. The motion picture projectionists' union has no record of an Albert Spinoza ever applying for membership in this state, but he did attend film school briefly at the University of San Diego; the program was brand new then, and they've preserved the early records. Pegler didn't know that, or he wouldn't have jumped to the conclusion that Spinoza had somehow heard about *Greed* when he was working at the Roxy in Pittsburgh. If he had known, he probably wouldn't have hired him, because an ignorance of film history would have helped Pegler keep his secret. Money was already tight — he was probably paying coolie wages for nonunion help. When he caught Spinoza snooping, he saw the gravy train ending for good once the secret got out. He flipped." She laughed without enjoyment. "The ironic part is he could have pled temporary insanity and probably walked."

"He'd still be guilty of extortion."

"Who from? You said von Stroheim died soon after. No crime has taken place when there's no one to press charges."

"His wife was his accomplice. She carried the body to the cellar and walled it up. She looked sturdy enough, Spinoza was small, and Pegler said she was handy at repair work. Then she plastered over the room next to the booth to conceal the evidence she'd overlooked."

"She was a loyal Old World–style helpmeet. Thank God they're extinct. She might've drawn a suspended sentence. She was dead within three years; of guilt, if you're poetically inclined. L.A. Medical Examiners office says it was ovarian cancer."

"I can't help feeling sorry for Pegler," Valentino said.

"I can. But then I'm trained to see past things like wrinkles and wheelchairs."

"The wrinkles were recent. If what he said is true, it was Erich von Stroheim's careless

326

smoking that robbed him of his legs."

"Filthy habit." She looked at her watch. He noticed nicotine stains on her first and second fingers. "Pegler should have sued," she said. "That's what civilized people do in these situations. But if you happen to be one of those benighted souls who favor punishment over rehabilitation — as I do — you can take comfort from the knowledge that Pegler's serving a life sentence at hard labor, reliving his crime over and over, every detail as fresh as the day he committed it. Hell on earth. Or at least in Hollywood."

"What about *Greed*?"

"If you mean that pile of gumbo in the evidence room, you can pick it up any time. The watch captain will give you a release."

"I mean the real thing."

"How about a ticket to the premiere? I assume there will be one. You owe me a good seat."

"You won't need it for evidence?"

"Of what? I said there isn't going to be a trial. Is it really ten hours long?"

"Eight or ten. But you said —"

"We've located a Spinoza cousin in Philadelphia; if he agrees to submit to a DNA test and it matches what we got from Mr. Bones, we can snap shut the file on this one. I'm not giving up my day off to appear against you on an interference charge that will probably just get thrown out of court."

"I'll get you as many tickets as you want," he said. "Bring all your friends."

"One's fine. I'm a cop." She tilted her head, and he realized what a beautiful woman she was when she wasn't pulling rank. "I'm curious about the picture. I've never seen one anybody was willing to go to jail for. That is, not since I left Vice."

"I'm free to go?"

"If you promise to confine your sleuthing to the area outside my precinct."

"I'll quit cold turkey."

"I won't even try to hold you to that. You and your friends had too much fun. Just keep it out of West Hollywood." She watched him get up and retrieve his jacket. "Speaking of friends, Harriet Johansen's finishing up the late shift in the lab. You can just catch her if you don't take the elevator."

CHAPTER 25

The sad stump of The Oracle's original marquee was dark. If any of the remaining bulbs were still functional, the wires to them had long since corroded or been chewed to pieces by squirrels. So many black snap letters were missing from GONE OUT OF BUSINESS that it had become a game among the neighbors to suggest answers to the puzzle: GO TO SIN was the winner so far. But today, as dusk drifted in under the diurnal stratum of smog, some of those neighbors may have found more entertaining speculation in the presence of lights burning on the ground floor after years of shadow.

Burning was the optimum word. In the lobby, which had been cleared of dust and rubble, dozens of candles flickered in colored glass bowls, casting a soft glow that fell short of the painters' and plasterers' drop cloths in the corners and of paint buckets shunted outside the range of the flames' heat. They stood on the floor and on stands and bordered a rich red carpet runner unfurled from the entrance to the doors leading into the auditorium. Kyle Broadhead watched Valentino lighting the last of them with a long taper.

"I hope you remember to blow those out," he said. "As picturesque as it might be for a film archivist to die in a burning theater."

"I'll remember." Valentino blew out the taper. In contrast to his friend's daily uniform of rumpled corduroy over a sweater-vest streaked with pipe ash, the film detective looked positively formal in a midnight blue suit and gray silk necktie. "I wish I'd thought to get scented ones. The place still smells like a tomb."

"Throw in a couple of cadavers and Harriet will feel right at home."

"One corpse was enough. Did you get the projector set up?"

"Almost. How much did you slip the electrician to wire the booth?"

"Leo Kalishnikov handled that part. I think it appealed to his eccentric aesthetic. We'll both be in trouble if an inspector happens by."

"No more than I, if they miss that projector before I can smuggle it back onto campus. Our department head frowns on borrowing six thousand dollars' worth of equipment for a private screening. But we're used to ticking off the authorities, aren't we?" He lit his pipe. "This ought to clear out some of the musk."

Construction was only ten days old, and already the building wore an air of industry. Sheets of blue tarpaulin protected the roof from leaks until it could be replaced, rotten plaster had been pulled down and drywall put up to substitute, winged Pegasus had been removed to a sculptor's shop for repair and to serve as model for a new mate to be built, and estimates were coming in from various artisans eager to take part in the restoration of woodwork, gold leaf, and custom fixtures. As they spoke, Kalishnikov, the designer, was in Texas, going over the plans for the new marquee with a sign maker who specialized in oversize projects. County and city permits were posted on the boarded-up windows in front. Valentino's savings and investments had already taken a hit of Peglerian proportions; soon he would have to tap in to the fifty thousand dollars his department head had parted with to obtain *Greed* for the archives. The check had changed hands with an outward show of reluctance that had failed to disguise the inner delight of both parties: The major find, on top of the solution to a grotesque and therefore sensational mystery connected with it, had brought a barrage of publicity to the film preservation program, and subsequently a large donation from an anonymous party (whose initials, appropriately, were *Q.T.*).

"Nice." Broadhead tested the thickness of the red carpet with a foot. "This should be out on the sidewalk. Haven't you ever attended a premiere before?"

"I was afraid someone would steal it. I have to have it back to the Hollywood Foreign Press before the Golden Globes."

The professor took something from his side pocket and held it out. It was wrapped in silver foil and tied with a red bow. "A housewarming gift. Fanta wrapped it. The number's the same, and it has some features your old one lacked."

The package was the size of a deck of cards. Valentino unwrapped it and opened the box. It contained a cell phone, smaller and sleeker than the one Broadhead had thrown out the window on the Santa Monica Freeway. "I'd say you shouldn't have," Valentino said, "but of course you should. Thank you."

It rang, raising two pairs of eyebrows.

"Probably the company," Broadhead said. "Telling you it's obsolete and offering to sell you a new one."

Valentino pulled up the antenna. "Hello?"

"Hey, Doc, you're killing me. Why didn't you tell me you were running a sneak preview?"

It was Henry Anklemire in Information Services. "How'd you find out about it?"

"I got sources. Listen, we need the bounce from when the story broke. You can't live on it forever; people forget. San Diego cops dug up a human femur in the old navy yard this morning. Dem bones of ours are dead as Pharaoh. I can put a photog out front in twenty minutes, get you the front page of the entertainment section."

"It's a private showing, Henry. Just for two."

"Romance! Hey, that's almost as good as murder. She take a good picture? Never mind, this guy can make Janet Reno look like Britney Spears. Tell her to show some leg."

"If a photographer shows up, I'll have him arrested for trespassing."

"That's cold. Here I am trying to help, and you set loose the Cossacks."

"Sorry, Henry."

Broadhead rolled his eyes and puffed up a

head of smoke.

"How about another one of those protest dealies?" Anklemire asked. "Any injuns in that picture?"

"None in the picture, and none out front. They packed up and went back to Berkeley when the police arrested Warren Pegler."

"That was a bust. He ain't even going to be tried. A week on Court TV's as good as thirty seconds in the Super Bowl."

"Good-bye, Henry. I'll let you know when we open the film to the public."

Broadhead watched him flip the phone shut. "Little twerp."

"Ten more like him and we could revive the career of Bull Montana."

"Are you sure you know how to handle that projector? I'd feel better if I stayed."

"I wouldn't. Three's a crowd. I can handle a projector."

"This isn't a sixteen-millimeter toy."

"I had a good teacher."

Broadhead bit down on his pipe. "Don't noise that around. They might expect me to teach more than two sessions a semester. Try not to touch the film. When you change the reels, don't forget to put on gloves. I left you a whole package in case you misplace a pair."

"If I misplace the package, I can always

borrow a pair from Harriet."

"Yes, she's sure to carry one in her date purse. You know you'll be jumping up every twenty minutes or so to change reels."

"That's why we're watching from the booth."

"You fixed it up nice. Comfortable bachelor apartment. Moving in?"

"Just for tonight. I don't have a certificate of occupancy."

"For what it's worth coming from an old widower, you made a fine catch," Broadhead said. "The shop talk alone should fill the awkward silences."

"Thanks, Kyle." He was moved.

Broadhead puffed vigorously. He seemed to be trying to build a smoke screen.

"Speaking of awkward silences," Valentino prompted.

The pipe came away; went back for another puff, then came away again. "I'm thinking of asking Fanta to marry me."

"Congratulations. She's as good a catch as Harriet."

"I thought you'd be surprised."

"I've been expecting something of the sort ever since you saw her in Michelle Pfeiffer's dress. You're not as inscrutable an old coot as you think."

"But I am an old coot. She had no trouble

convincing that gorilla at the Country Home I was her grandfather."

"She's a good actress. Dr. Zinnerman owes her an apology."

"Do your grizzled mentor a favor and forget I said anything. The idea's demented. I should check out that room."

"Why don't you ask her opinion? Over dinner, and wear something that doesn't look like you borrowed it from Sister Agnes in the Universal wardrobe department."

"Agnes needs to cool off before I go back there. You dropped that make-believe monocle so many times she couldn't see through the scratches." He shook his leonine head. "If anyone from UCLA sees me dating a student, I'll be out on my pension. It's marriage or nothing."

"You're an ornament of the university. No one forces ornaments into early retirement."

"Just between you and me, it's not that early. Very well, I'll ask her to dinner. Where do young people like to eat these days? Not one of those ghastly nightclubs, I hope."

"They go there to dance. Take her to the microbrewery."

"Ump. Romantic."

"I met Harriet at a crime scene. Our second date was an autopsy."

"We're a fine pair of academics, you with

your CSI beauty, me with my prom queen. Running around solving murders and haunting old theaters like the Phantom of the Opera. If Henry Anklemire were half the flack he thinks he is, he'd have us up to our mortarboards in paparazzi morning, noon, and night."

"I'm not an academic."

"Very well. Archivist."

"Not that either." Valentino pocketed his cell phone, took out a silver-plated card case, and handed it to Broadhead. It was engraved:

VALENTINO
FILM DETECTIVE

Broadhead sighed and handed it back. "One would think you were smart enough to save your money. That's a crystal doorknob for the ladies' lounge."

"You're not the only one who gives me presents." Valentino admired the case and put it away. "I got it from Harriet for my birthday."

"Your birthday was in July."

"We hadn't met yet. We're making up for lost time."

Broadhead's mouth formed something cutting. Then his face paled a shade.

"Fanta's birthday is next week. What do young women want these days?"

"How about a complete set of Agatha Christie?"

The professor went back upstairs to finish adjusting the projector. Alone in the lobby, Valentino saw that a candle had gone out. He lifted the taper off the empty candy counter, lit it from a candle, and stepped over a bank of tiny flames to reignite the wick. When he turned back, the taper burning in his hand, he looked into the stern face of Erich von Stroheim.

The director stood in the center of the red carpet with his feet spread in black boots that glistened to his knees, both hands folded behind his back. Tonight he wore the uniform of a high-ranking officer in the Austrian Imperial Guard, or what Valentino thought such a uniform would look like if he'd ever visited Vienna before the collapse of the empire; it was a dead ringer for the one von Stroheim had worn in *The Merry Widow,* down to the skintight black tunic paved with medals and crowned with epaulets and ropes of braid, and the spiked helmet fixed with a gold tassle that hung down to cover it completely, like the fezzes worn by Shriners. His monocle glittered, and candlelight twinkled on the rows of decorations from battles won and lost. His tan riding breeches showed every muscle in his powerful thighs; the old auteur had observed a military regimen of exercise in his prime. Valentino smelled polished leather; a new feature in these visitations. The others had been sight and sound only.

"Look," Valentino said, "you can stop pestering me now. The silver nitrate's here, and we've got it on safety in negative and positives in long-term storage. We're releasing it to theaters through MGM next spring. It'll be out on DVD in the fall. I don't know what else I can —"

A palm in an immaculate white glove swept out from behind the other's back and up, silencing him. It snapped down to his side, the thumb precisely parallel with the seam of his breeches. He stood motionless in that position for what seemed a full minute. Then he bowed, a short, jerky movement from the waist, no more than an inch. His heels collided with an explosive charge. He straightened and swept up his other hand. The braided leather riding-crop he held in it touched the visor of his helmet. It swished when he swept it back down.

The toe of one boot hooked itself behind the heel of the other, and with one movement, von Stroheim turned his back on his host and marched directly into the full-length stained-glass window in the wall. His squared shoulders and pinched waist blended with those of the Teutonic knight silhouetted on the panes and evaporated.

For an instant between the bow and the salute, Valentino thought he'd seen a tear gleam in the autocrat's naked eye. Surely he'd imagined that part.

"Are you interviewing ushers tonight?" Broadhead asked.

Valentino jumped. He hadn't heard him coming down from the projection booth. He blew out the taper and turned to face his friend standing in the auditorium doorway. "Not yet. It's way too early for that. Why?"

"Then who was the character in the uniform?"

"You *saw* him?"

"I couldn't miss him in that getup." He looked around. "Where'd he go?"

"I don't know, but don't tell Harriet."

She arrived by cab, wearing a simple black dress, high heels, and a white lace wrap covering her bare shoulders. Valentino opened the car door for her and paid the driver. They entered the lobby arm in arm. "You look beautiful."

"So do you. I wasn't sure about the dress. All these years in L.A. and I've never been to an opening."

"Not even with your negative cutter?"

She kissed him. It lasted fifteen seconds.

When their lips parted, she leaned back in his arms and used her fingertip to rub lipstick from his mouth. "That was to shut you up. You don't bring up old relationships on a hot date."

"I'd better get a booster shot, just in case." He kissed her.

He took her on a tour of the ground floor. She gasped when they entered the auditorium. The light coming from the square opening of the booth flattered the threadbare carpet and the rows of seats awaiting reupholstering. He'd spent all day dusting and polishing the woodwork and climbing up and down a stepladder with a broom, sweeping cobwebs out of the coffers. He'd had the shreds of the old linen screen removed and replaced with one made of a synthetic material that seemed to provide its own source of illumination. "I never dreamed you'd made so much progress," she said.

"Most of it's illusion. It's Hollywood, don't forget. The halfway point's still so far away you can't see it."

"Are you exaggerating?"

"You'll know I'm not when you find yourself using the gentlemen's lounge. They're still pulling asbestos out of the ladies'."

"What about your organ?"

He hesitated, searching her face in the reflected light. "The *pipe* organ! It needs new stops, a new pedal assembly, new everything. We evicted a family of mice from one of the pipes. A man's on his way from Chicago to dismantle it and put it right. He works for the company that made it originally. It's still in business; and so will the Oracle be, only not soon."

"Will you open it to the public?"

"I may have to, to cover the overhead. I haven't decided."

"Are you going to live here?"

He smiled. "Where better, for a professional film buff?"

"You'll never get away from the movies."

"The movies are where you go to get away from everything else."

She shook her golden head. "I have a confession to make. I've never seen a silent movie."

"What about those Rudolph Valentino shorts in Toronto?"

"We got in a fight during the first scene. I left."

"That's not so bad, as confessions go. You have to promise to see it again when it's scored. Silent films were never really silent. Dr. Broadhead's prowling the UCLA Music Department for a gifted young composer who won't charge us the farm." He opened the hidden door to the stairs. They started up.

"Is a skeleton going to fall in my lap?"

"If it did, you'd probably dust it for prints."

They entered the projection booth, which bore no resemblance to the gutted chamber of only a month before. Electric lamps cast a soft glow over a pair of armchairs from Valentino's apartment, a low round coffee table supporting a bottle of wine and two long-stemmed glasses, a figured rug, a sofa that unfolded into a bed. The massive air-cooled projector borrowed from the university stood sentinel at the opening into the auditorium, *Greed* stacked neatly in forty-two archival-quality cans on the floor beside it, the package of disposable latex gloves to hand. Harriet laughed when she saw the microwave oven and packets of unpopped corn.

Valentino started the film rolling and

joined her on the sofa, set on a raised platform to look down on the screen. She snuggled close to him and intertwined her fingers with his. He asked her where she'd been all his life.

"I know where I'll be the next eight hours."

"Or ten." He smiled.

CLOSING CREDITS

The following sources were instrumental in the writing of *Frames:*

Books

Technical

Cameron, James R. *Sound Pictures: Motion Picture Projectionist's Guide.* Woodmont, Conn.: Cameron, 1944.

The material is dated, but that was no hindrance to a story centered around a film shot eighty years ago. This updated edition of "the most practical book ever offered projectionists" appeared twenty-nine years after the first, with insights on the handling and presentation of nitrocellulose (silver nitrate) film, four years before the introduction of cellulose triacetate ("safety stock").

Kiesling, Barrett C. *Talking Pictures: How They Are Made/How to Appreciate Them.* New York: Johnson, 1937.

Dated also, Kiesling's entertaining text nevertheless dissects the Dream Factory at the height of its success.

Schary, Dore (as told to Charles Palmer). *Case History of a Movie.* New York: Random House, 1950.
  The movie, *The Next Voice You Hear,* is a dog; but Schary, head of production first at RKO, then MGM (Irving Thalberg's old job), provides an insider's tour of the moviemaking process from concept to public exhibition.

Historical

Architectural Digest, "Hollywood at Home" (various issues). New York: Condé Nast, 1990–2000.
  For many years a fixture at Academy Awards time, the swanky home magazine served up capsule biographies of stars, directors, writers, and producers classic and contemporary, with glimpses of their private lives and bushels of industry anecdotes — until cranky letters from color-photo fetishists persuaded the editors to discontinue the tradition.

Brownlow, Kevin. *Napoleon.* New York: Alfred A. Knopf, 1983.
  Brownlow's firsthand account of the

search for a complete print of Abel Gance's *Napoleon* reads like a Tom Clancy thriller, with a triumphant ending.

Brownlow, Kevin. *The Parade's Gone By.* Berkeley and Los Angeles: University of California, 1968.

This is the only indispensable source on the history of the silent film. Brownlow, a historian with matchless credentials (see Films: *Hollywood;* also the Acknowledgments), traces the evolution of an art form from its nineteenth-century beginnings to its annihilation by sound. His prose is both scholarly and eminently readable.

Donnelly, Paul. *Fade to Black.* London: Omnibus, 2000.

The author's a gossip, and in no small way a tabloid hack, emphasizing the lurid and sensational over the journalistic approach one would prefer; but his fat (633 page) collection of movie obituaries is handy for fast-track biographical research, as well as a helpful reminder of who's dead. Sort of a Who Was Who in Hollywood.

Drew, William M. *Speaking of Silents: First Ladies of the Screen.* New York: Vestal, 1989.

We should all thank providence for chroniclers like Drew and Kevin Brownlow, who have the foresight to interview Hollywood pioneers while they're still in a condition to reminisce. (Brownlow wrote the Foreword.) Legends Colleen Moore, Blanche Sweet, Laura La Plante, and others are no longer around to share the stories they tell here in first person.

Eames, John Douglas. *The MGM Story.* New York: Crown, 1985.
This entry in a monumental series on the major studios is a meticulous year-by-year history of the Tiffany of Tinseltown, 1924–1981.

Griffith, Richard, and Mayer, Arthur. *The Movies.* New York: Simon & Schuster, 1957; revised 1970.
The author of *Frames* learned most of what he still knows about the history of film through this huge volume, encountered at a very young age in first edition. Evidently, its authors are related to neither D. W. Griffith nor L. B. Mayer — but what fantastic billing!

Koszarski, Richard. *Von: The Life and Films of Erich von Stroheim: Revised and Expanded*

Edition. New York: Limelight, 2004.

Koszarski's earlier biography, *The Man You Loved to Hate,* was well received by critics and readers. About a third of this new incarnation contains additional and rewritten material: proof that Von Stroheim's reputation continues to grow. This early triple threat — actor/writer/ director — lived a life as colorful and dramatic as any of the characters he put through their paces before a camera, which if told on film would run at least as long as the original version of *Greed.*

Mordden, Ethan. *The Hollywood Studios: House Style in the Golden Age of the Movies.* New York: Alfred A. Knopf, 1988.

Mordden has a bitchy attitude; who but a Broadway gadfly cares if Fred Astaire's dialogue mixed up its theaters and performances in *The Band Wagon?* But his book dishes up a sharp and knowledgable comparison of Macy vs. Gimbel in Hollywood, as well as a fast-moving but richly detailed narrative of the rise and fall of the studio system.

Naylor, David. *Great American Movie Theaters.* Washington, D.C.: Preservation Press, 1987.

If you're looking for a plush folio to display on your coffee table, filled with mouth-watering pictures in full color, this isn't it. But being a National Trust publication, it's exhaustive, divided up by geographical locations, and formatted to slip into your pocket like a mushroom hunter's field guide. It's designed to travel, but you might want to book your reservations now. Not many of the popcorn palaces it celebrates are still standing.

Sinyard, Neil. *Silent Movies.* London: Bison, 1990.

A solid entry-level introduction to the revolutionary medium in its formative years, with concise narrative and many photographs.

Staggs, Sam. *Close-Up on Sunset Boulevard: Billy Wilder, Norma Desmond, and the Dark Hollywood Dream.* New York: St. Martin's, 2002.

It sounds like one of those fusty, pedantic snores penned for a Ph.D., with footnotes, but it's a lively, consciously cinematic presentation of the movie behind the movie, and the unlikely events that brought together a great director, a has-been movie star, a troubled leading man, and *two* (uppercase) Great Directors to create the most powerful and hypnotic Hollywood-on-Hollywood movie ever made. Aside from Gloria Swanson's brilliance as Desmond, this page-turner illuminates Erich von Stroheim's Max Mayerling as emblematic of the pathos of the Austrian's treatment by the industry. If you've seen *Sunset Boulevard* recently, it's like watching it all over again in a revealing new director's cut. If you haven't seen it in a while, or if you've never seen it, *Close-Up* will make you want to right away (see Films: *Sunset Boulevard*).

Film Guides

Halliwell, Leslie. *Film Guide.* New York: HarperCollins, 1977–present.

Halliwell was crotchedy, but correct in his details; a tradition that successors like John Walker continue to uphold. Just about everything one needs to know about just about every movie ever made is here, including the studio that made it — a detail most other guides overlook.

Maltin, Leonard. *Movie Guide.* New York: New American Library, 1970–present.

Maltin genuinely loves movies and it shows, but he's no toady, nor is anyone on his staff. His is the granddaddy of all movie guides, predating home video, when his readership was restricted to that curious species that set its alarm clocks for 2 a.m. to catch creaky old favorites on *The Late Show.* To keep the book a managable size, recent editions have jettisoned some listings, so it's a good idea not to throw away the older ones to make room for the new. (Advice to Maltin: Scrap the star index at the back for space. When you dropped Erich von Stroheim and kept Melanie Griffith, you destroyed its purpose.)

Fiction
Respectable writers of fiction don't crib from one another; but there's nothing like a well-researched, skillfully written novel on a chosen subject to inspire creation and saturate one in pertinent detail. Recommendations include:

Baker, James Robert. *Boy Wonder.* New York: NAL Books, 1988.
   This one's a ride, a satiric, seriocomic take on the contemporary industry tracing the meteoric rise and pile-driver fall of an *enfant terrible* producer. Like the movie *Network,* what first appeared as a riotously over-the-top sendup of American media looks like a sober documentary in light of more

recent events.

Fitzgerald, F. Scott. *The Last Tycoon.* New York: Charles Scribner's Sons, 1941.

At the end of his gaudy, rickrack life — burned out at forty-four — the author of *The Great Gatsby* reached back into the past and his experiences as a screenwriter to tell the only great insider's story of the bunker-like life of a brilliant studio executive, based on Irving Thalberg — burned out at thirty-seven. Tragically, Fitzgerald didn't live to finish the book. Sadder still, none has come along to equal it.

Kanin, Garson. *Moviola.* New York: Simon & Schuster, 1980.

Kanin *was* an insider: a phenomenally successful playwright, sought-after screenwriter (in tandem with his wife, actress Ruth Gordon), and close confidant of legends, including Spencer Tracy and Katharine Hepburn. *Moviola* is a delectable retelling — through the eyes of a fictional ancient studio mogul — of such items of cinema lore as the romance between Greta Garbo and John Gilbert and David O. Selznick's nationwide search for an actress to play Scarlett O'Hara in *Gone With the Wind.* There's a good deal more truth here than in many straight histories.

Roszak, Theodore. *Flicker.* New York: Simon & Schuster, 1991.
Until *The DaVinci Code* came along, there was nothing out there with which to compare this book. It's the story of a hunt for lost films, some of the technology involved, the netherworld of film societies and slasher geeks, subliminal messaging, and a conspiracy theory involving a cult made up of equal parts Shaker, Rosicrucian, and Turner Entertainment. Roszak's book got a bounce from Dan Brown's megaseller *Code* in the form of a reissue fourteen years after it disappeared below the radar.

ONLINE INFORMATION

Usually, this is an oxymoron. The Internet is unedited, and therefore less reliable in most cases than the Magic Eight Ball. However, Kodak has posted data on the Environmental Services page of its Web site essential to understanding the process involved in preserving, storing, transporting, and disposing of silver nitrate film, including molecular sieves and how to identify the dreaded five stages of decomposition. Details are absorbing and harrowing. The characters who stepped up beside Yves

Montand to truck nitroglycerine over a hundred miles of bad road in *The Wages of Fear* might have balked at this cargo. You'll find the site at — oh, something dot com. Just Google it.

Films

The following titles reveal, in terms this writer could never replicate, the beauty and drama of the silent film as it pertains to the career of Erich von Stroheim. Good luck finding some of them.

Foolish Wives. Directed by Erich von Stroheim, starring Maude George, Mae Busch, Cesare Gravina, and Malvina Polo. Universal, 1922.

Von Stroheim replicated Monte Carlo in astonishing detail for this melodramatic mix of seduction, blackmail, fakery, and murder. William Daniels and Ben Reynolds, who would later photograph *Greed,* taught their cameras to perform impossible feats. Available on DVD.

Greed. Directed by Erich von Stroheim, starring Gibson Gowland, Zasu Pitts, Jean Hersholt, Chester Conklin, and Dale Fuller. MGM, 1925.

Until someone actually discovers a complete print, we must make do with the four-hour reconstruction produced by Rick Schmidlin in 1999, using hundreds of stills and additional title cards based on Von Stroheim's shooting script. The effect, unfortunately, is static, and counterproductive to the epic poetry of the moving image. It still manages to astonish — and shock audiences misled to believe that the motion picture was family fare until the late 1960s — but sitting through it makes one long for Thalberg's two-hour cut. Available on VHS.

Hollywood. Produced by Kevin Brownlow and David Gill, narrated by James Mason. Thames Television, 1980.

Words cannot describe this thirteen-part series of one-hour documentaries on the silent film. Scenes from classics, beautifully remastered and projected at the original speed (not the herky-jerky comic pace that comes from running them through standard modern projectors), interspersed with personal accounts by pioneers who have since gone to the mezzanine in the sky, present a look firsthand at the birth and adolescence of an exciting new medium. It's another home run for Brownlow, with a healthy assist from David Gill, and an even greater achievement than *The Parade's*

Gone By. VHS, out of print.

The Merry Widow. Directed by Erich von Stroheim, starring Mae Murray, John Gilbert, Roy D'Arcy, Tully Marshall, and Josephine Crowell (cameo by Clark Gable!). MGM, 1925.

This is the one about the prince and the showgirl, based on an operetta by Franz Lehar, with the infamous boot-collection scene. (Von Stroheim: "He has a foot fetish." Thalberg: "And you have a footage fetish!") Not available on home video.

Sunset Boulevard. Directed by Billy Wilder, starring Gloria Swanson, William Holden, Erich von Stroheim, Cecil B. DeMille (cameos by Buster Keaton, H.B. Warner, Anna Q. Nillson, Henry Wilcoxon). Paramount, 1950.

Billy Wilder, another eccentric Austrian director, wrote this masterpiece under the indisputable influence of Raymond Chandler, with whom he collaborated on the script of *Double Indemnity* six years before. Ironically, it's the movie most people think of when they hear the names Swanson and Von Stroheim, made a generation after the dozens of pictures that made them household names throughout the world; but then that's the theme of *Boulevard:* No matter how much money you made for your studio and the industry, you're disposable and quickly forgotten. Von Stroheim's real-life fall from grace is eerily reflected in Max von Mayerling's subservience to the woman he'd directed and once wed. The casting is spot-on and unique. However eye-catching you find Andrew Lloyd Webber's musical stage adaptation in the 1990s, even his pool of talent couldn't approach an aging silent star cast as an aging silent star, a disgraced director playing a disgraced director, and DeMille playing DeMille. The film is the *Gone With the Wind* of cinema noir, and the best movie Hollywood ever made about Hollywood. Available on DVD.

ACKNOWLEDGMENTS

Frames could not have been written but for the inspiration and contributions of the following people, some of whom have exited the theater:

Bill Kennedy, host of *At the Movies.* For decades, Kennedy, a former movie bit player (*I Died a Thousand Times*) and radio announcer ("Faster than a speeding bullet! More powerful than a locomotive!"), introduced virtually the entire library of every studio afternoons on CKLW and later WKBD TV. His formidable knowledge of Hollywood lore — and his somewhat acerbic personality — required as much as fifteen minutes during station breaks while he fielded questions telephoned in by viewers. No one seemed to mind the interruptions.

Mary Morgan, hostess (with her dachshund, Liebchen) of *Million Dollar Movie.* This ladylike Detroiter, her hair piled high and sprayed hard as mahogany, brought a more genteel quality to local programming Sunday afternoons following Kennedy, scavenging features he'd overlooked.

Rita Bell, hostess of *Prize Movie*. On WXYZ Channel 7, infectiously bubbling Ms. Bell filled the time between reels taking calls from viewers trying to answer the trivia question of the hour. Each wrong answer added seven dollars to the cash prize awarded the winner.

Don Ameche, host of *Armchair Theater*. The urbane actor, whose career spanned sixty years (*The Story of Alexander Graham Bell, Heaven Can Wait, Trading Places, Cocoon*), brought style and polish to this network evening showcase, sipping cognac from a balloon glass and wearing a silk smoking jacket in the depths of a huge wingback easy chair.

The unsung programmers behind *Saturday Night at the Movies.* The Estleman family bonded around this weekly CBS fixture.

Deborah, the writer's wife. An accomplished novelist (as Deborah Morgan), she made suggestions, offered advice, counseled reason, and braved the terrors of the Internet to retrieve bales of technical material on preserving and restoring films photographed on silver nitrate. In addition, she holds her husband's hand through the closing credits long after everyone else has left the room.

Janet Hutchings, editor of *Ellery Queen's Mystery Magazine.* A friend and fine editor, she's published ten Valentino short stories as of the time of this writing. May this happy relationship continue.

The coveted final credit goes to Kevin Brownlow, author of *The Parade's Gone By* and coproducer of *Hollywood.* He's done more than any other person living to rescue the silent movie from oblivion and to raise the public consciousness to its appreciation; as a real-life film detective, he's recovered hundreds of miles of footage once considered lost, including the complete 235-minute cut of *Napoleon,* Abel Gance's 1927 epic — for whose 1979 premiere the eighty-nine-year-old director took his bows. In every way, Brownlow is the inspiration for Valentino. He may yet find *Greed.*

ABOUT THE AUTHOR

Loren D. Estleman has written more than fifty novels. In his illustrious career in fiction he has already netted four Shamus Awards for detective fiction, five Golden Spur Awards for Western fiction, and three Western Heritage Awards, among his many professional honors. He is currently working on *Alone,* the second Valentino mystery. He lives with his wife, author Deborah Morgan, in Michigan.

We hope you have enjoyed this Large Print book. Other Thorndike, Wheeler, and Chivers Press Large Print books are available at your library or directly from the publishers.

For information about current and upcoming titles, please call or write, without obligation, to:

Publisher
Thorndike Press
295 Kennedy Memorial Drive
Waterville, ME 04901
Tel. (800) 223-1244

or visit our Web site at:

http://gale.cengage.com/thorndike

OR

Chivers Large Print
published by BBC Audiobooks Ltd
St James House, The Square
Lower Bristol Road
Bath BA2 3SB
England
Tel. +44(0) 800 136919
email: bbcaudiobooks@bbc.co.uk
www.bbcaudiobooks.co.uk

All our Large Print titles are designed for easy reading, and all our books are made to last.